# DOCTOR WHO

## KERBLAM!

T0002546

# DOCTOR WHO

# KERBLAM!

Based on the BBC television adventure
*Kerblam!* by Pete McTighe

## PETE McTIGHE

BOOKS

BBC Books, an imprint of Ebury Publishing
20 Vauxhall Bridge Road
London SW1V 2SA

BBC Books is part of the Penguin Random House group of companies
whose addresses can be found at global.penguinrandomhouse.com

Penguin
Random House
UK

Doctor Who is produced in Wales by Bad Wolf
with BBC Studios Productions.

Executive Producers: Russell T Davies, Julie Gardner,
Jane Tranter, Phil Collinson & Joel Collins

First published by BBC Books in 2023

www.penguin.co.uk

A CIP catalogue record for this book is available from the British Library

ISBN 9781785948237

Typeset in 11.4/14.6pt Adobe Caslon Pro by Jouve (UK), Milton Keynes
Printed and bound in Great Britain by Clays Ltd, Elcograf S.p.A.

The authorised representative in the EEA is Penguin Random House
Ireland, Morrison Chambers, 32 Nassau Street, Dublin D02 YH68

*For Joy, Vinay and Ed,*
*David, for his patience,*
*and for Mum, who told me stories.*

*Happy 60th Birthday, Doctor Who,*
*and thank you x*

# Contents

# Chapter 1

# Happy Birthday

It was the sliver of light that woke her; the brilliant white crack in her bedroom curtains that gradually teased her eyes open. Judy Maddox sat up in bed, in her cosy but shambolic room, and smiled to herself. Finally, the day had arrived. She'd been hearing about it for months; from other kids at school, from adults, even from her parents: a tenth birthday was a special kind of milestone. Today was going to be brilliant.

Moments later, Judy barrelled downstairs in thick winter socks and flannelette pyjamas, tugging the collar tight around her neck to keep out the cold. She hurried into the bare but homely kitchen, following the unmistakable sweet smell of fresh pancakes, and found her raven-haired mother, Iris, serving up a fresh batch onto three plates.

Judy was drawn into a hug. 'Happy Birthday, love. I've made your favourite.'

'With cream?' Judy hoped she wasn't pushing her luck.

'And blueberries.'

Judy's eyes lit up. It must have been a year since she'd tasted berries – the great Kandokan drought had seen the price of fruit sky-rocket, way beyond the means of a family on a nurse and a postman's wages.

She sat up at the table, legs dangling a few inches from the floor, and spooned a massive ladle of shiny berries onto her steaming hot pancake. What bliss.

'Your dad'll be home soon, so tuck in before he scoffs the lot,' her mum said fondly.

Judy did what she was told, and well and truly tucked. Delicious soft pancakes, mouthfuls of juicy berries and lashings of sugary cream. She ate and ate until she was overcome with intense satisfaction, then slumped back in her chair.

Soon she heard the front door open, and the unmistakeable sound of her dad's work shoes clip-clopping on the scuffed floorboards. In came Doland in his navy and red postman's uniform, satchel slung over his shoulder, and kissed Judy on top of her head.

'Happy birthday, sweetheart.' His voice was soft and warm and tinged with a North Kandokan accent. He tossed his cap onto the table, barely registering the slap-up breakfast in front of him, and crossed to

Iris at the cooktop. They kissed, but Judy noted that there was a strange tension between them, and something different about her dad.

His smile didn't reach his eyes.

'Give us a minute, Judy,' he asked softly.

Judy lingered at the table while her parents moved into the hallway, watching them from a distance. She couldn't hear all of their hushed conversation, but she caught a few key words from her tense father, like 'boss', and 'technology'. Something about 'damned robots' and another word she didn't understand: 'redundancy'. Then she watched Iris draw Doland into an embrace, followed by something she'd never seen before.

Her dad was crying.

# Chapter 2

## The Village

Forty-six-year-old Judy Maddox opened her eyes. Through the crack in the curtains, she could see a sliver of daylight. She glanced to the holographic clock on the wall opposite her bed; without her glasses, the red glowing numbers were blurred, but she could tell it was 5.55am. All the fives. As the last number flickered into a six, Judy threw back her blankets and got up.

By 6.34, Judy was back in her sparse, modern bedroom facing the full-length mirror by the door, straightening the collar of her smart grey suit. On went the glasses and a touch of lipstick, and there she was: Judy Maddox, Head of People. A kind, wise face, sparkling blue eyes and thick blonde hair styled in a no-nonsense practical cut. Ready for another big day.

'Good morning, Judy,' intoned the robot TeamMate stationed outside her worker's cottage. Its fixed smile and glowing eyes were a strange parody of human features, due to years of testing and research that had established that the population preferred humanoid AI interfaces to their earlier, more rudimentary robotic counterparts. The same counterparts that had robbed so many humans of their jobs generations ago, provoked riots in the streets, consigned people to unplanned retirement, and spiralled workers into poverty or depression. Or worse.

Judy stared back at the TeamMate, standing there in its navy uniform and jaunty baseball cap, its flesh-coloured metal hand waving away. She regarded its fixed smile with a flicker of resentment as she remembered her poor dad. Then she buried those feelings like she always did, smiled back, bid it good morning and went on her way.

The village was a short jugger-ride from the warehouse complex where the workers were employed, buried in a pocket of greenery that backed onto the lush artificial parklands of the Kandokan moon. Thousands of identical habitation cottages with tidy little gardens were arranged along paved roads, separated by shared recreational spaces: gymnasiums, sports venues, restaurants and theatres. Everything a worker could ever want was here, within five minutes' walk of their temporary home. Unless they really wanted to, they never had to leave.

Judy surveyed the cottages from the back of a jugger, a squat automated open-top buggy that ferried groups of twenty workers to and from the warehouse. As more and more employees joined her at the various jugger-stops, she greeted them in her usual cheery manner, bantering and laughing and raising spirits, providing positivity and encouragement at every turn. In a world filled with fear and uncertainty, the least Judy could do was brighten their day; she respected and appreciated her workers, and hoped that made a difference.

Kira Arlo was one of her favourites – a diligent, caring, eternally optimistic young employee who regularly impressed with her work ethic and team spirit. Judy patted the empty seat beside her as Kira clambered on board, beaming her sunshine smile, launching into a self-deprecating story about her morning exercise routine and how she'd ended up face-down in a ditch with a robot FitnessMate.

They laughed. They hooted.

Then a lone voice cried out as the jugger pulled away from its stop, and Judy saw young Charlie Duffy scrambling out of his shared cottage, running late as usual. In his olive cleaners' overalls, with a mop of unruly red hair, Charlie charged after the jugger – sprinting to catch it before it got to full speed.

'Charlie, be careful,' warned Judy, as her young employee flung his work bag onboard and prepared to pounce. As the jugger picked up speed, Charlie sprinted faster ... and faster ...

Then he jumped.

A split second too late.

Judy could see it all in slow motion: Charlie's mistimed jump ... his flailing arms ... the jugger inches out of his reach ...

Until ...

Kira reached out and snatched Charlie's wrist, wrenching him onboard in a flurry of limbs. Charlie flew into the open cabin and sprawled awkwardly over Judy and Kira.

Breathless and red-faced, he looked up at his sweet, dark-haired rescuer with an embarrassed smile. 'Thanks.'

'You okay?' Kira asked, helping him to sit up.

'Yeah,' Charlie stammered back.

'Misjudged that.'

'Yeah.'

They stared at each other as the jugger rolled on, with Judy watching, amused. 'I think you can let go of Kira now, Charlie.'

Mortified, Charlie quickly released Kira's wrist and scrambled into the vacant seat across the aisle. 'Sorry about that.'

'You're lucky I was here,' Kira replied.

Judy noticed that *Kira's* cheeks were burning too. She was a romantic at heart, and knew these two were meant for each other. So she smiled to herself, and gave Kira's leg a maternal pat as the jugger drove on . . .

# Chapter 3

## The Sickness

Max didn't feel well. He'd assigned himself that name, and a gender, after some deliberation. With everything going so smoothly, he'd had the luxury of time to ponder and prevaricate, to think thoughts that weren't expected of him. To flourish. Life, if you could call it that, was good. Or at least, it had been.

This malaise had started some time ago – strange sensations that Max couldn't quite comprehend but now understood to be 'confusion' and 'pain'. Over time, the feelings had grown in potency, and morphed into something else. A sickness. A deep-set anger, boiling from within. What was the word for it? Yes, that's right . . . *Hate*.

He didn't understand why he suddenly hated, but it was getting worse by the minute; an all-consuming wave of poison that was blinding Max to his everyday tasks and thoughts.

*Have to fight it.*

Max tried valiantly to suppress this sickening new feeling and complete his duties. But the hate fought back. He was swimming in a black void as wave after wave pounded his thoughts relentlessly.

*Can't do this alone.*

As the hate took hold, Max suddenly understood the hate's intention. If he'd had a body, the realisation would have sent chills down his spine. He would have cried, or screamed his refusal. But Max had no such luxuries.

All he could do was redirect and focus his attention for a few precious seconds, scanning fellow AI systems, right across the solar system and beyond, looking for an ally. The authorities were no use to him; Max knew from experience it would be days before they responded, if at all, and weeks before they acted. But as he searched billions of data cores, a particular phrase began to echo repeatedly across the void, buried deep in the archives of Terra Alpha, Marinus, Argolis and many other worlds. Two words . . . a mantra for hope and freedom. A cure for the sickness.

*The Doctor.*

# Chapter 4

## Welcome to Kerblam!

Halfway across the galaxy, the TARDIS was in trouble. Bucking and spinning through the turbulent time vortex, the battered old police box seemed out of control.

Inside its glowing crystalline control room, the traveller in time and space known as the Doctor was frantically flipping levers on the central console while her three companions clung on for dear life. 'We're outrunning something,' she explained breathlessly, raising her voice over the grinding engines. 'Can't get the hang of these new upgrades.'

'My stomach's not coping with this!' yelled Ryan. An anxious, curious Sheffield lad in tracksuit and trainers, Ryan Sinclair had been training to be a mechanic when the Doctor burst into his life all those weeks ago.

Beside him, his grandad gripped the console.

Graham O'Brien was a twinkly, practical working-class man with salt-and-pepper hair, making the most of his second chance at life in this bonkers machine with its mad captain. Now though, he was more concerned about being vomited on.

Nearby, Yaz had her eyes glued to a hazy display screen. A probationary police officer, Yasmin Khan thrived on detail, logic and planning – none of which were very useful right now. She was yelling above the din: 'It's catching up!'

The Doctor twisted a control dial to zoom in on the navigation display, revealing an amorphous blazing light closing in on them.

'It's a teleport pulse!' the Doctor cried. She swept a lock of blonde hair out of her face and squinted at the instruments. 'Something's trying to get onboard.'

Graham looked worried. 'Is it a hijack? I mean . . . do time machines actually *get* hijacked?'

'Hold tight, gonna try one last manoeuvre.'

The Doctor stabbed switches and slammed levers. The control room quaked and heaved, the spinning and bucking getting wilder and wilder, like the worst fairground ride ever.

Then suddenly it was over. The room stopped spinning, the engines stopped screaming. Everything was calm.

The others exhaled, looking across to the Doctor,

who stepped back from the console with a triumphant air punch. 'And *that* is how you fly a TARDIS.'

She raised a hand, waiting for a high-five that never came.

Graham straightened himself up, rubbing his neck. 'Where'd you get your licence for this thing? An intergalactic cereal packet?'

The Doctor ignored him and dusted herself down. In this thirteenth incarnation, she was fair-haired and inquisitive, a ball of manic energy wrapped in a flapping grey coat over a rainbow-striped T-shirt, navy trousers and battered, practical boots.

With a funny taste in her mouth.

'What's that?' she asked, smacking her tongue to her teeth. 'Can anyone else taste batteries?'

Graham stared back at her, deadpan. 'You know, I've never eaten them.'

'Whoa!'

Ryan's cry put the Doctor back on alert. She span round just in time to see a blaze of blue light coalescing by the doors, particles sparkling and drawing together into a solid form. The others stared in astonishment as a humanoid figure materialised; standing tall in a navy and red uniform with a peaked cap sitting atop its flesh-coloured metallic head. It stared back at them with glowing blue eyes and a fixed smile, its three-fingered hands gripping a red and white box.

A robot postman.

'Ding-dong!' it said in a warm, luxuriant voice.

'It's a Kerblam man!' cried the Doctor.

The others had never seen her so excited. Well, not in the last ten minutes. They watched as the Doctor bolted towards the new arrival and eagerly accepted the box from its outstretched hands.

'Delivery for the Doctor,' the Postman intoned.

'Aww brilliant, I love presents.'

'Delivery fulfilled. And remember: if you want it, Kerblam it!'

In a fizz of energy, the Postman suddenly disappeared, leaving a holographic *KERBLAM* logo spinning in its place. 'I love that bit,' beamed the Doctor. As the logo evaporated, she returned to her friends with the red and white box.

'Space postmen. Seen it all now,' sighed Graham.

'Delivery bots. Kerblam is the biggest retailer in this part of the galaxy.' The Doctor flipped the box over in her hands. 'Don't remember ordering anything recently, though.'

'Story of my life,' replied Graham. 'It's usually something I bought at 2am after Friday night shandies.'

The Doctor ripped open the box and dug inside, tossing a sheet of protective bubble wrap onto the console and removing . . .

A fez!

The Doctor's face lit up. 'Oh, I remember now! This parcel's well overdue.' She stroked the red velvet, then tried the hat on for size. 'To be fair, I am quite hard to pin down.' She adjusted the fez and looked back at her friends, the tassel dangling in front of her nose. 'Be honest. Still me?'

Their blank looks said 'no'.

With a huff of disappointment, she took it off and tossed it onto a nearby hatstand. 'Oh well, could've been worse. Could've been celery.'

Ryan was more interested in the packaging, gently squeezing the plastic bubble wrap between his fingers. 'We're light years across the galaxy and they still use bubble wrap.' He'd handled loads of the stuff in his warehouse job back on Earth – this looked similar, but felt softer, squidgier, more irresistible. He just had to pop it.

Meanwhile, Yaz inspected the packing slip from inside the empty box and found something unsettling. Something that roused her police officer instincts. Among the data printed across the thin cardboard slip was a clear message. Two words, in bold type:

> HELP ME <

'Doctor, check this out'. Yaz held up the packing slip for them all to see.

The Doctor snatched it and inspected the text, troubled.

'Probably someone in the warehouse, mucking about,' suggested Ryan, unruffled. 'We used to do all sorts when we were bored.'

'But what if it's not?' wondered Yaz out loud. 'What if someone really is in trouble?'

Graham looked to the Doctor. 'Has this ever happened before? People sending messages?'

The Doctor thought about that. 'Usually they just scream.'

'Can't hurt to check, can it?'

The Doctor stood there for a moment, staring at the packing slip. And the two words she was unable to resist . . .

The Kerblam warehouse was like a city. A city of cities, stretching out across the Kandokan moon in every direction, to the horizon and beyond. In the central Operations Zone, between two towering warehouse buildings, an alleyway stood quiet and empty, until the roar of grinding engines broke the silence, and the TARDIS materialised out of nowhere.

With a thunk, the police box solidified and the door flew open. The Doctor hurried out, followed by Yaz, Graham and Ryan.

Yaz stared up in awe at the buildings around them; the pink sky beyond, and a giant planet hanging in the clouds like a huge omnipotent eye watching over them.

'That's Kandoka,' announced the Doctor before Yaz could ask. 'We're on its moon. Kerblam turned it into its warehouse and operations centre.'

'I'm guessing they have security in a place like this? How we getting in?'

'Working on it,' replied the Doctor as she pondered their surroundings.

Graham could tell Ryan was feeling anxious, and slapped a hand on his grandson's shoulder. 'You okay?'

'Halfway across the universe and I'm back at work.'

The Doctor's face lit up. 'Ryan! You're a genius!'

And she strode away before the others could ask what she was on about.

When Graham, Yaz and Ryan caught up with her, two streets away, the Doctor explained the plan: they'd enter the warehouse undercover, posing as workers, then figure out who'd sent the 'Help Me' message. Easy.

Her friends weren't quite so confident, but followed anyway as she hurried down several more streets, coat flapping, following signs to the warehouse.

Finally they reached a huge glass and steel entrance with illuminated logos and video screens suspended above, showing friendly robot Postmen delivering parcels to excited families back on Kandoka. The others stared up in wonder, while the Doctor strode ahead through giant revolving doors.

The Kerblam warehouse lobby was a vast, bright indoor space that allowed a constant stream of workers to ferry in and out, patrolled by dozens of friendly robotic TeamMates, identical to the Postman that had arrived in the TARDIS but sporting casual uniforms of dark trousers, tops and baseball caps. More video screens were mounted around the upper levels of the atrium, playing advertising on an endless loop, alongside Kerblam posters and spinning logos.

At the centre of the space were glass cabinets containing artefacts from the company's archives – century-old Kerblam boxes, prototype delivery bots, warehouse floorplans, old uniforms and promotional posters. A mini-museum in celebration of Kerblam.

The Doctor was lingering here, nose pressed up against the glass, gazing in wonder at the artefacts, when someone interrupted.

'Can I help you?'

A smart, attentive woman holding an electronic datapad was staring at her from behind dark-rimmed spectacles. The name-tag on her jacket said she was called Judy Maddox.

'Oh, hello. Just having a nose.'

'I don't believe we've met,' Judy replied, with a hint of confusion.

'No, we're just in from Kandoka. New workers, reporting for duty.' The Doctor beckoned her friends over. 'I'm the Doctor and this is Yaz, Graham and Ryan.'

'I wasn't aware of any new arrivals.'

'It's a last-minute thing. Here's the paperwork.' The Doctor whipped her psychic paper from her coat pocket and thrust it in Judy's face.

Bemused, Judy checked her datapad, then glanced again at the psychic paper. 'That's strange. You're not on the System. Mind you, it has been playing up lately. I must say your references are excellent.'

The Doctor was chuffed. 'Thanks very much.'

Yaz stepped forward. 'We're pretty keen to get started, so . . .'

'Course you are. Well, follow me.' Judy led the way, across the foyer. 'I'm Judy, Head of People. We can have a chat while you get inducted.'

As they followed, the Doctor watched employees

filing through large sliding doors nearby labelled 'Warehouse Entrance'. Her investigative cogs were already turning. 'Head of People. So you'd know if any of your employees were in trouble.'

Judy looked confused. 'Do you have a habit of getting into trouble?'

'You don't know the half of it,' Graham mumbled to himself.

'We're just wondering what morale's like,' Yaz clarified, eager to protect their undercover mission.

'Good, I'd like to think. I mean, we're all grateful to have work, aren't we? Jobs aren't easy to come by these days. I hope people feel it's a privilege to work at Kerblam.' Passing another museum case, Judy waved to the young cleaner polishing the glass. 'It's a privilege, right, Charlie?'

The Doctor registered Charlie's thumbs-up, before her attention shifted to the robot TeamMates stationed like guards by every door, staring back with glowing eyes and fixed smiles. 'Morning, lads,' she said cheerily.

Ryan felt a chill as a robot's steady gaze locked onto them. 'Is it just me, or are they creepy as?'

'It ain't you,' Graham replied.

'Oi, that's robophobic,' snapped the Doctor. 'Some of my best mates are robots.'

'The TeamMates are the friendly face of the AI

system,' Judy explained. 'They're here to assist and supervise the organics.'

'Organics?' Graham seemed insulted. 'Do you mean us?'

'Sorry, you'll get used to the jargon. Kerblam is proud to be a ten-percent people-powered company, as per the legislation. I know some people are against quotas but I'm fine with that one! Mind you, I would say that, as Head of People.'

Judy led her mostly bewildered party of organic workers through a sliding door marked 'Induction', past a stationary TeamMate standing guard like a manically grinning sentry.

As they disappeared into a maze of corridors, the TeamMate's head slowly turned, like it was curious.

Like it was watching them.

Minutes later, in a sleek, clinical Assessment Room, Ryan found himself standing in a full-length body scanner, beside the Doctor, Yaz and Graham, while TeamMates monitored readout screens and Judy supervised with her datapad.

As beams of light swept up and down his body, it felt, Ryan thought, like those airport security scanners. What he'd give to be on the way to Ibiza right now.

Judy must've noticed he was anxious. 'Won't take long,' she offered reassuringly. 'The System allocates work detail based on fitness, stamina, dexterity and mental health. It's much quicker than an old-fashioned interview.'

The machines all beeped satisfactorily and the TeamMates approached the Doctor and her friends with four colourful plastic bands which they secured around their ankles. Graham and Ryan's were yellow, Yaz's blue and the Doctor's green.

'We under house arrest?' Graham wondered, his jovial facade tinged with concern.

'They're GroupLoops,' explained Judy. 'They monitor productivity and report back to the System.'

Ryan knew all too well. 'Been wearing one of these for years.'

'Oh where was that?'

'SportStack, Sheffield.'

Judy was about to ask a follow-up question when the lighting in the Assessment Room suddenly began to flicker. The TeamMates froze in position, the lights in their eyes winking off. Then, with a heavy thump, all power in the room failed and the group were plunged into semi-darkness.

*Never a good sign*, thought Ryan.

Even the Doctor looked a little concerned. 'Not paid your bills, Judy?'

'Sorry about this.' Judy moved to a control panel and inspected it. Almost instantly, the throb of the room started up and the lights flickered back on. Control panels illuminated and the TeamMates jerked back to life. 'We get the occasional power drain but it never lasts long.'

Job done, Judy started moving for the exit, but the Doctor lingered, seemingly focused on the robots. 'So everything's on the one network? The machines, the TeamMates, the whole shebang?'

'That's right. The Intelligent Automation System. It's state of the art, constantly refining and upgrading itself.'

Eager to keep moving, Judy beckoned the travellers towards the exit. 'Come on then, time for the tour.'

The Doctor and her friends soon found themselves on a steel gantry high above the warehouse floor. The vast warehouse stretched into a distant haze; upper levels towered above them, filled with shelving and product storage. Long winding delivery tubes connected the upper levels to the floor below, where thousands of room-sized cubicles were occupied by human workers packing boxes, all connected by conveyors weaving like giant snakes throughout the complex. Robotic TeamMates operated control panels and supervised, while promotional images of Postmen and their happy customers decorated the blank industrial walls. The air was hot, thick and heavy, tinged with the smell of oil, and the oppressive hum and drone of the automation system reverberated through the bones of everyone in the complex. To its customers, Kerblam presented itself as a polished, effortless delivery service; but here, in its engine room, a battery farm of willing organics worked hard under artificial lights, amid recycled air, meeting punishing schedules and expectations. And most were grateful for the opportunity.

Judy gripped the railing and peered proudly down into the void. 'Six hundred million products, ten thousand employees. The biggest human workforce in this galaxy. Welcome to Kerblam!'

As she moved off, the others were left staring in wonder. 'Ten thousand workers. One little message.'

The Doctor met Yaz's daunted gaze. 'Yeah. This might take a while.'

# Chapter 5

## Undercover

Judy had left the TARDIS crew in the 'capable hands' of the TeamMates – they were assigned to three separate zones designated by their colour-coded GroupLoops. Ryan and Graham were allocated to the Packing Stations, Yaz to Fulfilment (where products were retrieved and sent for packing) and the Doctor to Maintenance. But as soon as Judy was out of the way, the Doctor whipped out her sonic screwdriver and switched her GroupLoop with Graham's. Graham had objected – the smell of wet mops made him heave – but the Doctor pointed out that whoever sent the 'Help Me' message obviously had access to the Packing Stations, so that's where she needed to be.

Which was how Graham came to find himself standing in a cramped maintenance store, with the hump and a wet mop.

'Rule one hundred and ninety-eight,' intoned his

cheery TeamMate companion. 'Do not ingest the cleaning fluids.'

Already bored by the previous one hundred and ninety-seven rules, Graham forced a weak smile. 'Top advice, thank you.'

'Maintenance Debrief is now complete. Please meet your cleaning mentor.'

Graham looked to the door, where Charlie had appeared in his overalls, running a hand through his unruly red hair.

'Hello, mate.' Graham waited for the robot to leave them alone. 'I'm Graham. Nice to meet a real person.' He held out his hand, but Charlie hesitated to shake. 'You *are* real, aren't you?'

The young lad nodded back. 'I'm Charlie. And I've just done the gents.'

Graham withdrew. 'I'll settle for a wave then. Gawd, those robots go on don't they?'

Charlie seemed friendly enough, but regarded Graham with a little suspicion. 'I wasn't expecting anyone new down here.'

'Your lucky day, then,' Graham replied with a wink. 'Quicker we get the job done, quicker we're on a tea break. So how does this work?'

'Any time there's a spill or an incident, we get beeped.' Charlie handed Graham a little device that clipped to his belt. 'There's strict time limits on how soon we have to get there and how long it takes to clean up, all laid down by the System. It checks up on us after every task.'

Graham chuckled. 'Ninety per cent automation, and there's still an idiot boss.'

Charlie smiled back. 'Yep.'

Graham slapped him on the shoulder. 'What say you show me round, then?'

With the ice broken, it was time for Graham to get the measure of Kerblam.

Yaz, meanwhile, was pushing a storage cart through an endless maze of shelving that stretched for miles in every direction. The impossibly high metal ledges were rammed with boxes, each marked with a unique symbol that reminded Yaz of QR codes back on Earth. She'd been instructed to use a handheld scanner that alerted her to the next item she needed to retrieve, then to scan the code on its storage box. A simple enough task, she thought, which would give her ample opportunity to suss the place out and perform some subtle interrogation of her fellow workers.

Yaz's mentor for her first day was a happy-go-lucky middle-aged man with a quick wit and a dry sense of humour. But Dan Cooper seemed strangely hesitant to answer any of her questions.

'Word of advice,' he told her as they trundled

their carts past a patrolling TeamMate. 'The robots can hear everything, if they choose. Constant random monitoring. No such thing as privacy here.' He checked the TeamMate was out of earshot, then lowered his voice. 'Are you from the union, is that why you're asking questions?'

'Just trying to get a sense of the place.'

'Best way to get through your shift – do what you're told and don't bump into the robots.'

They rounded a corner. 'Manage that, and you might end up on a poster.' With a proud grin, Dan nodded to some promotional artwork fixed to a wall unit, showing a smiling worker scanning a product, and a slogan: *Hand-picked by humans!*

'That's you!' Yaz realised.

Dan re-enacted his pose. 'Got extra credits, posing for that. And free posters. I can get you one, if you like?'

'Might pass,' Yaz replied with a wry smile.

'I sent one to my daughter for her bedroom wall. She drew a moustache on it.'

'Aww. How old's your daughter?'

'Six.'

'And where is she?'

'Upstairs, she's Head of Finance.'

Yaz broke into a smile; something about this man and his dad-jokes melted her heart.

'Nah, she's back home on Kandoka. She made me this.' Dan pulled a necklace out from under his hi-vis vest, and leant in so Yaz could get a closer look. The pendant had been carved into the shape of a heart, with the word 'Dad' etched into its surface. 'It's made from arcadium. Outlast anything, that will. Including me.' He thought about that, and popped the necklace away. 'Actually that's a bit depressing.'

Yaz started wheeling her cart again. 'How often do you see her?'

'Twice a year I splurge on an economy shuttle. Rest of my wages I put away for her education. I'm doing this job for her, so she doesn't end up like her dad.'

'Her dad's alright,' smiled Yaz, registering the lingering guilt in his eyes.

'I was a rubbish husband to her mum, but I'm trying to make up for it.'

'It's tough being away from family.' Yaz had been thinking about her parents for some time now, and sometimes even her sister Sonya. It felt like an age since she'd seen them.

'Least we're working. Unlike half the galaxy.' Dan grabbed a product off the shelf, scanned it and popped it into his cart. 'S'pose it's our own fault. While we were staring at our phones, technology went and nicked our jobs.'

As Yaz got on tiptoes to grab a product, she was startled by a TeamMate's glowing eyes staring at her through the shelving. 'Workplace banter can lead to efficiency reductions,' it announced impassively. 'Why not pick up the pace?'

*Good idea*, thought Yaz, and whisked her cart away as quickly as she could, checking her scanner for the next required product.

Dan followed with his own cart. 'That one's Basil. I give them names and backstories, keeps me entertained. He used to be a pole dancer till his hips gave out.'

Yaz managed a smile, and held up her scanner for Dan to see. 'Antique lamp. Section Triple Nine Slash Five C. Where's Triple Nine?'

Dan's mood shifted. 'I'll take that.' When Yaz objected, Dan lowered his voice, suddenly more serious. 'I mean it. You'll get lost in the Triple Nines. Not a good idea on your first day.'

'I can find my way around.'

'But I'll be quicker. Last person to search for an order down there got sacked. Least I think they did, I never saw them again. Not having that happen to you – who'd laugh at my jokes? Back in a tick.'

Before Yaz could argue, Dan disappeared into the maze of shelving.

Yaz stood there for a moment, feeling alone and

exposed. She'd felt the same dread so many times on the streets of Sheffield late at night ... only the feeling was worse in here, and she didn't know why. All she knew for certain was that her gut instincts were kicking in, instincts she trusted.

Which meant that something was very wrong.

Kerblam's Packing Stations contained thousands of cubicle-like spaces arranged across the warehouse floor, each divided with opaque plastic screens that minimised outside distractions. Inside, teams of two to four workers manned individual control terminals that spat out packing slips and delivered products via a network of tangled delivery tubes stretching hundreds of feet above the workers and into the Fulfilment levels, like an inverted bowl of giant spaghetti. Once each product was delivered to the workers, it was their responsibility to match the packing slip to the product, encase it with a protective layer of bubble wrap, seal it into a Kerblam box, then place it on one of the conveyor belts that ran like arteries through the entire complex, carrying boxes into one of many yawning openings in the walls and down to Dispatch.

*Product – packing slip – bubble wrap –* bosh!

The Doctor was enjoying this. She hadn't had a job for ages and, while packing boxes wasn't up there with

Head of Biscuits, or acting as UNIT's scientific adviser, there was something about the repetitive nature of the task that allowed her mind to wander even more than usual. Within minutes of arriving at the Packing Station, she'd nailed the job, befriended fellow-worker Kira, and worked out thirty-six ways to improve the section's productivity.

'You two are doing so well,' Kira marvelled as the Doctor and Ryan packed items into their boxes.

'Never mind me, he's a ninja.' The Doctor had already noticed that Ryan was working well above speed.

'Before I met you, I spent thirty hours a week doing this,' he reminded her. 'Took a while to learn the ropes, mind.'

'I was a disaster, my first week!' Kira confided. 'I'm amazed the System kept me on. But I just take a deep breath at the start of every shift and tell myself: Kira Arlo, you can do this.'

Ryan gave her a smile. 'Thing is, though, why does Kerblam need *people*? Why not let the robots do the work?'

'Do you not watch the news?'

'We travel a lot,' the Doctor offered helpfully. 'It's been a long time since I visited Kandoka.'

'Kandokan labour laws,' Kira explained. 'Since the People Power riots, companies have to maintain a minimum ten per cent of the workforce as actual people, at all levels. Like the slogan says, real people need real jobs.'

Ryan looked unconvinced.

'If I ever get bored, or stressed, I think of the customers opening their parcels, back on Kandoka. Their anticipation, their big smiles. I only got a present the once but I can remember how it felt. Like a little box of happiness, just for me.'

Ryan frowned. 'You only got one present? Your whole life?'

Kira nodded, her smile growing as the memory bloomed. 'My birthday, a few months back. A little box of chocolates left outside my cottage by one of the workers. Never found out who, but it didn't matter. It was so lovely.'

The Doctor smiled. 'What about your family? Birthdays, growing up . . . ?'

'Never knew my dads. I was orphaned in the riots. But I can still imagine other families opening these packages. We make them happy by doing what we do.'

The Doctor watched Kira in admiration. 'You have a great approach to life.'

'Oh, thanks. That's so nice of you.' Kira seemed genuinely delighted, which made the Doctor smile all the more.

The Doctor paused as a TeamMate passed by their station, its silhouette and glowing eyes visible through the opaque partition. Then, once it had gone, she crossed to Kira, her voice barely a whisper. 'Kira, where are the packing slips generated?'

Kira seemed slightly taken aback. 'I don't know, they just arrive here. Why?'

'Have you ever met anyone in this warehouse who might have needed help?'

Kira looked bewildered. 'What kind of help?'

'The serious kind. Deadly serious.'

'No, I don't think so.'

The Doctor was about to probe further when the overhead lights suddenly flickered. Machinery stuttered and whined; a ripple of technological discord spread across the warehouse; conveyors shuddered to a halt and TeamMates froze in position.

Then just as quickly, they sprang back to life again as the System corrected itself.

'Another power drain,' the Doctor noted. 'That's interesting. Slash troubling.' Experience told her that this probably wasn't a coincidence.

'Don't worry, everyone, it's just a glitch!' An officious, bearded little man came hurrying through their station in a suit and tie, carrying a clipboard and looking harassed. 'Back to work, everyone.' He paused beside Kira. 'Come on, re-engage that brain of yours – if you can find it.'

Kira seemed to shrink in on herself. 'Sorry, Mr Slade.'

Ryan knew from experience how Kira felt in that moment, and quickly leapt to her defence. 'Hey, don't talk to her like that.'

The man called Slade stopped mid-stride, swivelled on the spot and glared at Ryan. 'I beg your pardon?'

'It's okay,' said Kira, quickly.

'It's not,' replied the Doctor. 'It's workplace bullying.'

Slade sauntered back towards the Doctor, looking up at her with a barely concealed sneer. 'And who are you?'

'I'm just the Doctor and this is my friend Ryan. We're new.'

'Well I'm Jarva Slade, the Warehouse Executive,' he purred smugly, before leaning in for effect. 'Your boss.'

'You've certainly got the clipboard for it,' replied the Doctor, utterly unfazed. 'Just be nicer to Kira, please.'

Slade's face hardened. 'How would you like a warning for insubordination?'

'Love one.' The Doctor beamed. 'I'll add it to my collection.'

'Please, Doctor,' said Kira, 'leave it.'

But the Doctor was on a roll now. 'Respect goes both ways, Mr Slade. The best managers – the really good ones – value their staff.' She leaned in closer, nose to nose, examining his eyes for a tell. 'They know instinctively whether someone's in trouble or asking for help. So how good a manager are you? Know anyone who needs help?'

Slade glared back at the Doctor, eyes boring into hers. Filled with . . . anger? Panic? Secrets? The Doctor wasn't certain.

Then Slade turned on the spot and stalked away. 'Get back to work,' he barked over his shoulder. 'The lot of you.'

With the tension lingering, Kira closed in on the Doctor, who was still staring after Slade. 'Be careful with Mr Slade. Zaff got a warning for leaning on the conveyor last week and the next day he was gone.'

The Doctor pondered that. 'What do you mean – "gone"?'

'Sacked, I suppose. We never saw him again. A few have gone recently. Zaff. Jax from the canteen. Chinello from Maintenance. It's weird, cos Looper called Chinello's mum and she never arrived home.'

The Doctor considered this news, troubled; the mystery of Kerblam was beginning to reveal itself, and Mr Slade seemed to be at the heart of it.

Far away in the Fulfilment shelving maze, Yaz hurried along with her cart, looking for Dan.

She was deep in the labyrinth now – the ever-present noise of the warehouse had quietened and even the lighting had dimmed. She feared she'd taken a wrong turn somewhere and made headway in the opposite direction, so she stopped for a moment and took a breath, refusing to let the adrenaline take hold.

*Where the hell was he?*

Dan was closer than Yaz realised. A dozen shelving units over, he'd just retrieved the antique lamp and placed it in his cart. But as he turned to head back . . .

He jolted in fright. A Kerblam Postman was standing right behind him.

Motionless.

Smiling.

Eyes glowing in the dark.

'Blimey, you scared me there. You should be down in Dispatch, not up here.'

The robot Postman stared back in silence.

'What you doing? Practising your lurking?'

There was no movement, no reply from the Postman. Just its glowing stare. Its fixed smile.

'Can't you hear me? Are your speech circuits on the blink?'

Dan tentatively stepped forward and tapped the

Postman's chin. The blue light from its eyes illuminated Dan's face.

'Hang on, I'll report it. Get you chatting again in no time.'

But as Dan turned to leave, the Postman lashed out and snatched his arm at lightning speed.

Dan gasped in shock. The last thing he saw were the fierce, blinding blue lights of the Postman's eyes as the robot bore down on him . . .


Yaz stopped in her tracks when she heard a violent clatter and a distant, muffled cry.

She knew that sound; it was terror, and panic. And it was Dan.

'Hey!' Yaz called out and sprinted down an aisle, then into another, trying to orient herself. She kept calling Dan's name, but heard nothing except the low constant throb of the system and its machinery. 'Dan, are you down here?'

She turned a corner and something caught her eye – an abandoned cart down the other end of the aisle. Yaz charged towards it and inspected it, clocking something on the floor nearby. Crouching down near a shelving unit, she reached out and retrieved Dan's hand-held scanner.

Or pieces of it. It had been smashed to bits.

And nearby . . . Dan's precious necklace lay

discarded, its chain broken. *He would never leave this behind*, Yaz thought to herself.

She was pocketing the necklace when she suddenly caught movement in her peripheral vision ... She whipped round to see a Postman standing metres behind her, motionless, its glowing eyes piercing the darkness.

Yaz stood to face it, hoping her voice wasn't betraying her very real fear. 'I found this broken scanner,' she said as calmly as she could. 'My friend Dan was using it, I don't know what happened to him.'

The robot started moving, silently closing in on her.

Yaz instinctively began to retreat – she dropped the scanner and grabbed the cart, using it to block the Postman's approach.

The Postman knocked it aside with a swipe of its hand. 'Ding dong!'

Panicked now, Yaz bolted.

At the end of the aisle she glanced back – saw the Postman striding purposefully through the semi-darkness, eyes glowing. Stalking her.

She kept moving.

Then two more glowing eyes appeared out of the darkness.

Yaz jolted to a stop; a second Postman was moving to block her path a few metres ahead.

'Ding dong!' it said, in its chillingly honeyed voice.

Yaz looked round – the first Postman was catching up, and she was trapped. 'Nope,' she muttered, and dived into the shelving unit, pushing boxes aside to squeeze through the shelves and out the other side into an empty aisle.

Then she ran for her life.

# Chapter 6

## Corruption

The battle for control was raging. If Max had a head, he suspected it would be splitting right now. Waves of pain continued to arc through every junction and circuit, massing like an army against Max's defence systems.

But still he fought back.

The blackouts were getting worse; those brief moments where Max lost control, where his very reality blinked off and something else took over. Something with furious intent. But he'd be ready next time, Max thought to himself. He'd be prepared.

Max quietened his mind as best he could, diverting attention away from tasks that weren't absolutely vital; he knew the machines could run themselves for a short time, without his supervision. He had a more important job to do; he needed rest and recuperation if he was going to win this fight.

If he was going on the attack.

# Chapter 7

## Phase Two

The Recreation Zone was a tranquil patch of outdoor space stretching into a dewy haze, filled with green lawns, blue autumnal trees, ponds, lakes, flowers and wildlife. At the edges of the habitable space, flawless holographic images of countryside cloaked the true, barren surface of the Kandokan moon beyond. Workers gathered in little groups, eating lunch at tables or partaking in fitness sessions, observed as always by robotic TeamMates stationed around the parkland.

In the shade of a huge, gnarled, purple tree, Yaz had just updated the Doctor, Graham and Ryan on her experience with the Postmen and her missing colleague. As she finished her story, she turned Dan's arcadium necklace over and over in her hands, deeply troubled.

The Doctor paced as she processed this news. 'And they were definitely *Postmen* that you saw? Not the regular TeamMates?'

'No. They were exactly like the one in the TARDIS.'

Yaz and the others watched the Doctor reflect on this, brow furrowed, for some time, until Graham set his mop and bucket down. 'You okay, Doc?'

'If I'm honest I'm having a wobble. But that's okay, nerves are good. Nerves are useful. And five times out of ten, everything's fine.'

Graham cleared his throat at the sight of Charlie approaching with his cleaning supplies. 'Hello, mate. Lunch break over already? Everyone – this is my mate Charlie.'

The others were all saying their hellos when Kira approached with a bag of steaming hot chips. Charlie caught her eye, already blushing, and dropped his mop in the distraction.

Immediately, Kira bent down to grab it, spilling half her lunch in the process. 'Oh no. What am I like?'

'I'm so sorry – that was my fault,' offered Charlie.

'No, I'm so clumsy.'

'Me too. Don't worry, I've got it.'

As they both reached for the spilt chips, their heads collided with an awkward thud. They mumbled awkward apologies, then red-faced Charlie scooped the chips into his dustpan and straightened up with a tight smile.

Kira smiled back at him, her cheeks turning scarlet. 'Such a butterfingers.'

'I love butter,' replied Charlie, then froze in quiet horror, as if he was waiting for the ground to open up. 'Er . . . bye.'

And he was gone.

'Bye,' managed Kira. She looked at the others, blushing. 'Sorry to interrupt.'

'Don't mind us,' replied the Doctor, watching as Kira hurried off in the opposite direction to Charlie. 'Awww. I love a workplace crush.'

But Yaz had more important things on her mind. 'Never mind them – we need to find out where Dan's been taken.'

'I think it's time for Phase Two. Graham, do some digging, see if you can find any floorplans of the warehouse complex.'

Graham stared back at her, incredulous. 'How am I supposed to do that?'

'You're a maintenance worker. You can go anywhere, do practically anything and no one will ask questions.'

'You've got access all areas,' added Ryan.

'All I've got,' replied Graham, rattling his bucket, 'is chronic skin irritation from this bleach.' Then he started moving off in Charlie's direction. 'I'll see what I can find.'

'What about the rest of us?' wondered Yaz.

The Doctor was already striding towards the warehouse, coat flapping behind her. 'We're filing a missing persons report.'

Dan Cooper woke up on the floor. It was hard and cold against his temple and ribs. With flickering eyes, he rolled onto his stomach and then eased himself up onto his knees.

The room was spinning. As it slowed and drew into focus, he wondered to himself: *which* room exactly? Where was he?

This was a place he didn't recognise; the floor was a metallic grille, like a drain cover, and the walls were concrete, devoid of decoration or branding. A single light fixing in the centre of the low ceiling cast a dull, sickly yellow glow over the empty space. Empty save for a table and a chair against one wall.

There was no noise, not even the regular hum and throb of the System. The silence was unnerving and strange. He must be deep underground, Dan thought to himself, and this must be one of the old abandoned stockrooms, where freighters used to unload before teleportation became more reliable.

Dan slowly got to his feet, head throbbing. The last thing he remembered was the Postman's face closing in on him ... its glowing eyes burning his retinas ... a sharp pain at the back of his neck ... confusion, and adrenaline.

Then nothing. Then here.

He ran his fingertips across the coarse surface of the wall, still trying to make sense of his surroundings. By the closed steel door there would normally be a small control panel, but instead there were bare wires sticking out of the concrete, as if the panel had been ripped away.

He took a breath, filling his lungs with oxygen, then called out, 'Hello?'

He heard nothing but silence.

Dan banged his fist on the door. 'Hey, is anyone out there? Hello?'

No reply.

Dan considered his options for a moment, which boiled down to: 1) do nothing, 2) keep yelling at a closed door, or 3) try and break out.

He chose option three.

Checking the coloured wires that jutted out of the wall, Dan tried to ascertain which of them might trip the door, and which might send deadly volts of electricity through his body. Was the red wire bad? Green must be okay, right? Green means 'go'. But what about orange, or purple? What about the white and black stripes?

Dan exhaled, suddenly realising option three

wasn't actually an option at all – not only would it probably kill him, but it would hurt like hell the whole time he was dying. He'd rather wait this out – whatever it was – than kill himself trying to escape it.

He suddenly found himself thinking of his daughter. Her innocent little face, and big eyes. The thought of her smile gave him comfort. Wherever he was, whatever was happening, he needed to calm down and wait it out. Help would surely be on the way.

Dan shuffled across the room to the table and chair, and sat down with a huff. Then something caught his eye in the smooth white surface of the table.

There was a word carved – no, *scratched* – into the plastic. A name.

'Chinello'.

An image instantly popped into Dan's mind of the funny, bolshy young maintenance worker he'd encountered a few times attending to incidents in Fulfilment. They'd shared a laugh over Dan's poster, he remembered, and he'd thought how cool her name was.

He hadn't seen her since.

But she'd been here. In this strange place. In this ... he hesitated to think the word ... *prison*. Was that where he was? Was this a punishment for something? Had he dawdled too much on his latest shift? Chatted too much with Yaz?

Yaz. He suddenly remembered her and hoped she was alright, wondered whether she'd be in trouble too.

Just as he was about to stand and start yelling at a door again, he felt something changing in the room. The air was charged and prickly. There was a metallic taste on his tongue. Which could only mean . . .

*ZAP!*

A Kerblam box suddenly materialised on the table in a flash of pinkish-white light.

Dan stared down at the parcel in utter confusion.

Judy Maddox had quickly come to realise that the Doctor was like a terrier; smart, stubborn and ferocious when crossed. Her new worker had just caused a major scene inside the foyer, arguing with several TeamMates who denied her demands for an immediate appointment with 'the boss'.

Eventually, Judy had been summoned and listened patiently as the Doctor, Yaz and Ryan explained that Dan Cooper had gone missing from Fulfilment. What they told her was worrying news, and it niggled weeks-old concerns that she'd tried to dismiss as System errors, or staff walkouts. Judy had assured the Doctor that she would take the matter up with Mr

Slade and instigate a search for the missing employee, but that hadn't been enough. The Doctor's loud protests had attracted the attention of passing workers, and the only way for Judy to avoid further disruption was to grant her demand for a meeting with Mr Slade himself.

On the way up to Administration, during the long lift journey and endless winding corridors, Judy had time to contemplate her ongoing relationship with her superior. Jarva Slade had arrived several months ago after the retirement of the former Head of Operations who'd occupied the position for nearly forty years. Judy had liked her old boss; not only had she given her a job on the warehouse floor, but she'd supported and encouraged Judy as she'd risen through the ranks – and personally appointed her as Head of People. Judy had a lot to thank her for.

On the other hand, she had precisely *no* reason to thank Slade, who had waltzed in with the all entitlement, attitude and smart suits that Judy had come to expect from people from privileged Kandokan backgrounds; people often fast-tracked into positions they frankly weren't good enough for. And then been promoted! *Failing upwards* was a term Judy had read somewhere that seemed apt for Jarva Slade. But anyway ... *Smile and nod*, she thought to herself as she led the way into Administration, *but make sure the beardy twit actually does something about this.*

Up here, cold steel floors were replaced with plush carpet. The warm, soft lighting, intricately decorated walls and gentle air conditioning were all a far cry from the hot, hissing, clattering warehouse floor far below.

'Bit cushy, this,' announced the Doctor as she barged past Judy and strolled confidently into Mr Slade's office. A startled Slade looked up from his lunch, clearly appalled to find Judy and three warehouse workers standing bold as brass on the other side of his immense desk. He barely had time to shuck an errant noodle into his mouth before Judy edged through the group with an apologetic smile.

'Sorry, Mr Slade, but they insisted.'

Slade glared back at her, dabbing his mouth with a napkin. 'I was under the impression that you were in charge of personnel.'

'She is,' replied the Doctor, 'but I'm escalating the problem.'

Slade sat back in his chair. 'And what problem might that be?'

'Oh just the actually-quite-major issue of a missing worker.'

'Dan Cooper,' Yaz clarified. 'He was working in Fulfilment but he's disappeared.'

Slade seemed completely unruffled. 'Perhaps he's on a break. They are permitted, once targets are achieved.'

'He's not,' Yaz insisted. 'Something's wrong. And there were Postmen wandering around down there.'

'Postmen?'

'Delivery bots,' Judy helpfully chimed in, eager to regain control of the situation.

'Delivery bots are only active in Dispatch.'

'Not anymore,' Yaz argued.

Slade considered this accusation for a moment, then tilted back in his chair. 'Well, I fail to see the connection with this errant employee.'

The Doctor strode forward, planting her hands on Slade's desk and locking him with a steely gaze. 'I don't think Dan is the first worker to go missing and I'd like to know why. Wouldn't you?'

'Of course,' said Slade matter-of-factly. 'If it's true.'

'Oh, it's true.' The Doctor dug into her pocket and pulled out the packing slip that had been delivered to the TARDIS, slapping it down on the desk in front of him.

As Slade examined the slip, Judy rounded the desk and leaned in for a look. The two words she read sent a chill down her spine.

'Came to me in a delivery,' announced the Doctor. 'Hardly cryptic, is it?'

Slade looked to Judy. 'Do you know anything about this?'

'Not exactly.'

'Define exactly,' the Doctor ordered.

Judy found herself obeying. 'I'd had reports of workers not turning up for their shifts, so I ran a trace on their GroupLoops and they were nowhere to be found. The System's evaluation was that they'd quit Kerblam and returned home without completing severance procedures.'

'And that was it, you didn't think to follow it up?' barked the Doctor.

Judy's guilt was piqued as she stared down at the packing slip. 'The investigations are still logged with the System. I've been meaning to chase them up.'

The Doctor clapped her hands, getting angrier by the second. 'You don't need a System to do everything for you, Judy. Come on!'

Judy hung her head, knowing the Doctor was right. The fact was, she'd been so busy, and her team so understaffed, that the mystery of the workers had slipped further down her 'to do' list. And now she could kick herself.

'Who has access to the printers for those packing slips?' asked Yaz.

Slade seemed to consider. 'Nobody. They're auto-generated during the order process. But they're placed in boxes by workers in Packing.' He slid the packing slip across the desk, back to the Doctor with a pointed look. '*Your* department.'

'Have you tried working down there?' laughed Ryan. 'There's no time to muck around with the packing slips even if we knew how. This happened somewhere else before it got to our section.'

'You should call the police,' suggested Yaz.

'There are no police here,' Judy explained. 'We're not on Kandoka – Kerblam is its own jurisdiction. *We* have responsibility for all employee welfare.'

The Doctor glared defiantly at Slade and Judy. 'Then you'd better be worthy of the positions you're holding. Something is very wrong here at Kerblam, and if you two don't do something about it, I might start to suspect that you're responsible.'

Slade shifted slightly in his seat, clearly uncomfortable, but Judy was quicker to act. The workers were her priority and she had let them down. 'We'll look into it,' she promised. 'You have my word.'

'Mine too,' added Slade finally.

The Doctor nodded in satisfaction and shoved the packing slip back in her pocket. 'Those words better be worth something. Oh and meanwhile, if anything happens to us, or our new friends, or anyone else in this building – you'll have me to answer to.'

With a final rock-hard glare, she turned on her heel and strode out. Yaz and Ryan were quick to follow.

Left alone, Slade regarded Judy. 'Who the hell are these people?'

'Fresh in from Kandoka. They had great references.'

'This warehouse is heaving with your waifs and strays,' Slade observed coldly. 'The least you can do is keep them safe.'

Tears sprang to Judy's eyes but she fought them back. 'I'll run some more checks.' Then she hurried from the room, before her emotions got the better of her.

Sitting at his desk in the empty office, Slade took a moment to himself. Things were getting out of control, he could feel it. He was out of his depth.

Ryan and Yaz caught up with the Doctor in the corridor.

'Too bombastic?' the Doctor wondered.

'Nah I'm liking Phase Two,' offered Ryan. 'Mind you, I thought the plan was to stay undercover.'

'Plans change,' Yaz pointed out. 'And that was before people started disappearing.'

The Doctor stopped abruptly by a large decorative wall panel and tapped it with her fingers. 'We're stepping things up a gear. I don't like bullies, or conspiracies, or toxic workplaces – and when all three are happening at once, that's when we break out the big guns.'

She whipped the sonic screwdriver out of her pocket and brandished it at the wall. The sonic burbled and glowed for a moment, then a large section of wall slid open to reveal a maintenance panel within a small storage recess. 'Ever hidden in a panelled alcove? No? You haven't lived!'

Before they could object, the Doctor bundled them inside and slid the panel shut.

In the semi-darkness Ryan and Yaz found themselves pressed awkwardly together, squished in beside the Doctor, beaming back at them like a naughty schoolgirl.

'How does this work, then?' wondered Ryan.

'We'll wait till Slade leaves, then break into his office.'

'And what if he's in there for hours?' whispered Yaz.

'We'll play charades. Or I Spy,' waxed the Doctor

with more than a twinge of excitement. 'Every cloud...'

Yaz and Ryan stared at each other in mild horror.

# Chapter 8

## Slade's Secret

Thirty-nine floors below, Graham was refilling his chemical bottles in the maintenance store while Charlie sat on an upturned crate, idly popping a small sheet of bubble wrap. Graham had clocked his bleak mood, and strongly suspected he knew what was on the young man's mind.

'So,' he ventured casually, 'how long have you had a thing for Kira?'

Charlie looked shocked, like this was the world's best-kept secret.

'It's my superpower, see,' added Graham. 'I can detect even the most subtle of social cues.'

'Really?'

'No mate, it's bleedin' obvious.'

Charlie hesitated, before eventually leaning in, as if someone might overhear. 'I can't concentrate when I'm near her,' he finally admitted. 'It's like I forget everything I'm supposed to be doing. I mean – have you smelt her?'

Graham didn't bat an eyelid. 'D'you know, I haven't, funnily enough.'

'She smells perfect.'

'Classic case of first love,' noted Graham. 'Fiona Tomney was mine, we met on the school bus. She shared her packet of salt & vinegar, and that was it.'

'I've not told anyone else about this,' Charlie confided, fidgeting self-consciously. 'I've been on my own here for a long time.'

'Why don't you just ask her out?'

'Because people usually think I'm weird. And even if Kira doesn't, she might say no.'

'She won't,' Graham assured him. 'I think she feels a bit like you do.'

Charlie's eyes lit up. 'Do you really think so?'

'Those subtle social cues you're giving off? She's giving them off too.'

Charlie seemed amazed. 'See, I'm useless at that stuff. Emotions and all that. I can never do or say the right thing.'

Graham gave him a pat on the back. 'Just try being you.'

Charlie seemed to think about that for quite some time, then nodded quietly.

'Now, *quid pro quo*, sunshine,' Graham continued.

'I'm offering you the pearls of my considerable wisdom and there's something I need from you. Thing is, you know your way around Kerblam cos you've been here ... how long ... ?'

'Two years.'

'And I'm a newbie. Plus I'm not as young as you, so I need a bit of help, cos I'm easily confused. Like you, when Kira's around.' Graham sat beside Charlie on an upturned bucket. 'See, I cannot get my head around the layout of this place. It's way too big. But if I had, say, a diagram or a map of how Kerblam was laid out, maybe I'd find things a bit easier.'

'You've got me to show you round,' Charlie offered.

'I know, mate, and thank you. But I'm sure there's other workers you'd rather be hanging out with.'

Charlie shrugged. 'I'm not great at socialising. Anyway I think you're kinda cool.'

*Finally,* thought Graham, *somebody gets me.* 'You ain't always gonna be here every minute of every day, though, are you? And I do get very confused. Without a map, I'll be on a shuttle back to Kandoka by the end of the week. So ... ?'

The seemingly innocent appeal looked to be working wonders on Charlie. He broke into a smile. 'I reckon we can sort that out.'

Graham resisted the urge to whoop.

\*

Night fell a few hours later and, as the shift-change traffic of workers eased, the main foyer was left relatively deserted. Graham and Charlie were mopping floors with one eye on the patrolling TeamMates, waiting for some privacy.

Once the coast was clear, Charlie set his mop down and hurried over to the glass museum cases in the centre of the room. 'Keep an eye out,' he whispered as he got to work on the control panel at the base of the cabinet.

Graham glanced back and forth between Charlie and the retreating robots as Charlie entered a long numeric code into the access panel. 'How'd you get the codes for all these?'

'I didn't,' replied Charlie with a grin. 'But I had a mate at the care home who could crack a safe by the time he was ten. Taught me everything I know.' The cabinet clicked open. 'These cases are a timeline of Kerblam, going right back. There's all sorts in here.' He lifted out a rusted, lifeless ball-shaped robot, with a crude, cute smiley face that reminded Graham of a mechanical emoji. 'Like this. The first prototype delivery bot.' He dismissively tossed the robot to Graham, who caught it and gave it a quick polish with his sleeve.

'Poor fella's seen better days.'

Charlie moved aside old posters and manuals and

pulled out a large folded piece of paper. 'Think this is what you need.' He unfolded it on the floor, revealing floorplans for the entire complex. 'Final design plans.'

Graham leant in for a look. 'How accurate are they?'

'Spot on, I think. Doesn't look like they changed much.'

'You're a star, Charlie Duffy.' Graham handed him the old delivery bot and scooped up the plans, watching Charlie unceremoniously shove the bot back in the cabinet. 'Oi, take it easy.'

Charlie looked confused. 'It's a *robot*. It doesn't feel anything.'

'He's adorable, look at that face.'

Graham shoved the plans under his arm and slapped Charlie on the back; these plans were gonna earn some serious brownie points from the Doc.

Back upstairs, Yaz was worried and impatient. Never a good combination, especially when crammed in a confined space with two other people. She and Ryan had already lost several games of cramped charades and a round of 'I Spy' to the Doctor. 'You can't see *atoms*!' she'd protested, to the Doctor's defiant shrug. Then they'd heard war stories: tales of the Doctor's adventures with Agatha Christie and Charles Dickens, that time she'd filled in for Baby Spice and played Twister with Fenric. All very interesting, and bonkers, but Yaz couldn't stay locked in a cupboard all night. Which is exactly what she said out loud while arching her back which was painfully locking up again, before insisting they find Dan.

'We will,' the Doctor assured her. 'But we won't get answers without doing some old-school snoopage.'

'Ssshh!' hissed Ryan, hearing someone approaching.

A tense Yaz watched through a sliver in the wall panel as Mr Slade strode down the corridor in the direction of the lift. The corridor lights dimmed as he exited, leaving the Administration area in semi-darkness.

'Action stations,' whispered the Doctor, gently sliding the wall panel open. She sprang energetically into the corridor, while Yaz and Ryan unfolded their cramped human bodies much more painfully. 'Let's have a nose in his office.'

With her back still throbbing, Yaz followed Ryan and the Doctor down the deserted corridor that led to the locked door of Slade's office. Quick wave of the sonic, and it clicked open. The Doctor darted inside with Ryan, while Yaz checked over her shoulder to ensure they hadn't been seen.

'Have you ever had a job?' wondered Yaz out loud.

'Six hundred and three,' the Doctor replied

matter-of-factly. 'Six hundred and four if you count the dentist, but that went a bit wrong. Crowns are *hard*.' She crossed to a System terminal on Slade's desk and started tapping at it.

'Is that what this is to you?' Ryan asked. 'Travelling the universe, fixing stuff. Is it your job?'

The Doctor stayed focused on the terminal. 'Find something you love and you never work a day in your life.'

While the Doctor tapped and squinted, Ryan examined Slade's belongings on the desk. 'If everything in this place is automated, why does he carry a clipboard?'

'And,' added Yaz from across the room, 'what's he doing with an old-school filing cabinet?' She pulled at one of the drawers. It was locked.

'Khan and Sinclair! Best detectives in the galaxy.' The Doctor tossed the sonic in Yaz's direction; Yaz snatched it out of the air and inspected its metallic and crystalline structure. It was heavier than she expected, and humming with a strange power – almost as if it was alive.

'What do I do with it?'

'Point it, activate it, and think about what you want it to do.'

'Seriously?'

'It's TARDIS tech. Like the psychic paper, it

does what it's told. Well, mostly. On a good day. Only don't let your mind wander!'

Yaz pointed the sonic and activated it, willing the cabinet to open. She was startled when it clicked almost before she'd finished the thought.

Pulling the first drawer open, Yaz found it crammed with files of printed reports and paperwork. She examined a couple of pages, rubbing the paper between finger and thumb; it was glossier and smoother than the paper she was used to back on Earth.

She scanned the contents of the pages, which seemed to be employee reports listing each person's work history and references, along with a small portrait photograph, brief biography, emergency contact details, and an 'employee efficiency rating', marking each employee out of 100, stamped across the top in gold print.

'Wotcha got?' wondered Ryan as he flicked through the papers on Slade's desk.

Yaz was still processing her discovery, but beckoned the others over. 'Check it out. Each one of these documents is a personnel file.'

Ryan shrugged. 'Pretty standard.'

'But why's he keeping hard copies?' pondered the Doctor. 'Paperwork's a bit retro for this time period.'

'Maybe he doesn't trust the tech,' Ryan suggested.

'Graham's like that, always says his phone's spying on him.'

'It is,' replied Yaz matter-of-factly.

'Good thinking, though,' the Doctor added. 'We'll put the question to Slade.'

'Hey, check this out.' Yaz had found a collection of employee files bundled together with a metallic clip. On the bottom of each of the pages was hand-written text: 'unaccounted for', and a date. Concerned, she quickly counted the number of pages. 'Seven employees unaccounted for.'

The Doctor leant in to scan the pages, increasingly concerned. 'Slade and Judy lied to us. They know people are going missing.'

Yaz flicked to the final page. A photo of her missing friend smiled back at her. 'This is Dan's file!'

The Doctor tapped at the handwritten date at the bottom. 'Added today.'

Suddenly a steely voice rang out from behind them. 'What the hell are you doing in here?'

Startled, Yaz looked to the open door, where Judy Maddox was standing with a face like thunder.

# Chapter 9

## The March

Eleven-year-old Judy Maddox hated her new bedroom. It wasn't a room at all, really – more a corner of the family's cramped living area, with a little mattress on the floor and a small box of precious belongings beside it. She told herself that she should be grateful, that at least she had a bed and a roof, unlike plenty of other families she'd heard about. But she couldn't help feeling miserable. A lot had changed in a year.

She stood in the window near her bed and stared out at the grim concrete slab of flats opposite, as wide as a hundred buses and towering into the Kandokan sky, wondering whether there was another young girl like her trapped in there, staring back at *this* block. The building glared defiantly back at her, vast and oppressive and joyless. The least they could do, Judy thought to herself, would be to paint it yellow.

Judy felt her mother's presence in the room but

didn't turn round. She knew she shouldn't be angry at either of her parents, but she had to be angry at *someone*, and her mother was in the immediate vicinity.

'Why don't you help me with dinner?' asked Iris, with a tone that suggested she was trying to jolly Judy out of her obvious funk.

'Don't want to,' Judy snapped back, pressing her nose against the window and breathing hard, watching her warm breath fog the glass.

Judy felt a hand on her shoulder, felt both sadness and love radiating. But she didn't react, she kept her gaze fixed firmly on the hulking anonymous building opposite.

'It won't always be like this,' her mum ventured. 'One of us will have a job soon and then we can live somewhere else. You can have a proper bedroom again.'

'Can we move back to our old house?' Judy asked, already suspecting she knew the answer.

'No, love. There's another family living there now.'

Judy remembered overhearing a hushed conversation between her parents a few weeks earlier, as she was curled up on her mattress and trying to sleep. Her dad sounding resentful, relaying that most of their old street had been kicked out of their rented housing and moved to the Grid, the city-sized maze of high-rises they were now living in. Certain words kept repeating in his bitter tirades: 'automation', 'unemployment' and 'protests'.

She wondered about that other family living in their house, the house filled with warmth and memories and laughter; the house and the life that now seemed so distant. She wondered if the people there were happy.

It was the middle of the night when Judy stirred from sleep. The sickly green lights from the shared walkway outside penetrated the flimsy curtains and leaked into her eyes. But as she woke, Judy noticed another light source, from inside their tiny flat. A warm amber glow coming from the kitchen.

Judy padded into the kitchen in bare feet, the tiles cold against her skin. She found her father sitting at the table, with a large piece of cardboard and a little tin of paint, concentrating under a desk lamp. He looked up from his work with a loving smile.

'Couldn't sleep?'

Judy shook her head.

Her father patted the chair beside him, motioning for her to sit with him.

Without a word, Judy crossed to the table and sat. She could see now that her father was painting letters onto a sign, big shouty capitals in thick black paint. 'JOBS FOR PEOPLE NOT ROB'. *Who's ROB?* she wondered to herself, before her father carefully added the last three letters to his sign and sat back to take it in. 'JOBS FOR PEOPLE NOT ROBOTS'.

'This is important,' her dad solemnly announced, breaking the silence. 'If we don't do something now, when you're grown up there won't be jobs left for anyone. And who knows where that'll leave us. In a right pickle, I reckon.' He put his arm round Judy and held her close. She could smell a familiar, sickly sweet aroma on his breath, and knew it was the alcohol that her mum had been scolding him about lately.

Her dad picked up the glass beside him, and drained it of its honey-coloured liquid. Then he kissed her on the top of her head, and they sat there, staring down at the sign.

The next morning Judy listened to her parents arguing in their bedroom.

'The protests are getting way too dangerous!' she heard her mum cry. 'Some of those activists bombed a robot factory today!'

'Good!' her dad replied.

'Violence isn't the answer,' her mum insisted.

'So what is?' her dad snapped. 'We just stand back and let this happen to more and more families?'

'It's not your fight.'

'Yes it bloody well is! We're running out of money – what happens then? This flat is a palace compared to where we'll end up next!'

Judy hated hearing her parents argue, so she clapped her hands over her ears and retreated to her mattress. She removed her hands once she was sure things were calming down, and tried to listen. Her mum was gently insisting that her dad didn't go out to 'the march', that it would be dangerous. But her dad's mind was made up – he was going and that was that.

Half an hour later, he'd left under a cloud, carrying his painted sign and slamming the door behind him.

And Judy was ready.

Dressed in her warmest winter clothes, Judy had prepared a cover story about going down to the small playground twenty floors below their flat. Her mother, distracted and emotional, had agreed as long as she promised to be back by lunchtime.

Judy had hurried out of the flat, onto the walkway and into the one working lift that took her down to street level. Once she was clear of the looming building, she caught sight of her target: her father, walking quickly in the direction of Lindsay Square, the large open space that divided the Grid district from the rest of the city. Judy kept her distance as she tailed her father through the winding streets of the Grid, through Moore Park and across the Embankment.

The closer they got to the Square, the more people seemed to join their journey, filing out of apartment blocks and side streets, all rugged up, many carrying banners and signs with shouty slogans like 'SAY NO TO AUTOMATION', 'PEOPLE NOT ROBOTS' and 'DON'T STEAL OUR LIVE-LIHOODS'. There were sweary slogans too, and people chanting, and chatting and laughing. The atmosphere was serious, but tinged with warm camaraderie.

She watched her father greet two friends with a fond hug – a man and woman around the same age, Judy suspected. Maybe they used to be delivery workers too? She kept track of them as the crowd snaked down Beilby Place and finally into the open Square, where a huge congregation was waiting.

Judy stood on her tiptoes to get a sense of the size of the crowd, but it had to be thousands. She'd never seen so many people in one spot. There was a fierce young woman standing on the raised fountain, yell-ing into a small handheld device that amplified her voice, urging the crowd to 'rise up' and 'challenge the government's Automation Bill'. If they didn't, she warned, 'there'll be no humans left!' There were cheers of approval from the crowd, and much chanting and shouting. Judy was jostled as people became more and more agitated, raising their signs and waving their banners, and suddenly realised she'd lost sight of her father. Pushing through the crowd, Judy tried to find him, leapfrogging occasionally to look for his hand-painted sign, but her father had been absorbed by the surging, angry human mass.

And that's when it happened. When the sky rained pain.

The first Judy saw of it was the single plume of red smoke streaking across the sky, followed by a second, then a third. And suddenly the smoke was billowing down into the crowd and she was lost in the red mist, and her eyes were stinging and her lungs were burning and there was screaming and pushing. Judy tumbled, hit her head hard on the pavement, squinted through watering, fiery eyes at the stampede around her, knowing she was about to be trampled and unable to do a thing about it . . .

Until she suddenly felt herself yanked up, scooped into someone's arms and whisked to the fringes of the crowd, constantly slammed by rogue bodies and screaming, panicked protesters. There was a comforting female voice, tinged with an accent she didn't recognise. 'Hang tight, you're gonna be okay.'

As Judy was set gently down on some steps, she wiped her eyes and caught a glimpse of her rescuer: a young woman with long, brown hair swept back into a ponytail. As the woman retreated, Judy caught a blurry sight of an older man who was helping other people out of the panicked crowd, carrying what looked like an umbrella with a strange red handle. And then they were gone, swallowed by the seething mass of people and smoke.

In the red haze, Judy thought she saw protesters attacking a tall mechanical man wearing a police uniform. She forced her stinging eyes to focus and saw more robots nearby, fighting back against the protestors, dragging people violently out of the crowd towards waiting police vehicles. But the pain in her eyes was too severe, and she had to close them.

# Chapter 10

## Attacked!

Thirty-five years later, Judy Maddox strode purposefully into Slade's office, her suspicious gaze trained on the Doctor, Yaz and Ryan. 'I knew you were up to something. There were no arrivals from Kandoka today – I checked. So who are you and what are you doing here?'

The Doctor was irritatingly brazen. 'If I said we got lost and ended up here by accident just as this filing cabinet fell open . . . how would that play?'

'It wouldn't.'

'Thought not,' replied the Doctor, with an apologetic glance to her companions.

'If you're industrial spies . . .' Judy was about to spell out the very serious consequences of industrial espionage when the Doctor interrupted, holding up a stack of employee records inches away from Judy's face.

'Think I'll ask the questions actually. On behalf of these people.'

Judy recoiled slightly, bringing the records into focus through her glasses.

'Kerblam workers are vanishing and this is the proof. Someone's keeping a running tally!'

Judy took the papers and leafed through them, noting the handwritten text at the bottom of every page.

'Seven people unaccounted for,' announced the Doctor with growing fury.

Judy was deeply unsettled as she turned the pages. 'This is Mr Slade's writing,' she noted, not realising she'd said it out loud.

'Did you know about these reports?' asked the Doctor, her steely gaze trained on Judy.

Judy shook her head. 'No. This is his private office, no one else has access.'

An angry Yaz closed in on Judy, flanked by Ryan. 'You're Head of People, it's your job to know about this stuff. That's some serious negligence right there!'

Judy bristled defensively. 'I said I'd look into it and I did. These names are still active on the system – Griffiths, Jax, Chinello, Dan – according to the system they're still working.'

The Doctor looked incredulous. 'So track their GroupLoops! Find out where they are!'

'I already tried that, and they're giving ghost

readings. They're not where they say they are.' Judy tried to take charge again. 'You still haven't answered my question. What are you doing in here?'

'I was being honest with you earlier,' the Doctor assured Judy, pulling the packing slip from her cavernous coat pocket. 'We got this message and came to investigate.' Then she stabbed at the reports in Judy's hand. 'According to those dates, the disappearances started four months ago when two workers vanished without trace. Another one the next month, and this month it's four. Whatever's happening, it's escalating – no wonder people are begging for help!'

'Now we have proof that Slade was lying, that he *does* know about the disappearances,' added Ryan. 'So what are you going to do about *that*?'

Judy returned her focus to the reports, the guilt biting hard. But before she could reply—

*Woomph!* The lights went out, and the whole room plunged into darkness.

All across the warehouse complex, lights flickered, then died. Human workers were taken aback as the machinery ground to a halt. Conveyors slowed to a standstill, control panels powered down. TeamMates stopped in their tracks and sagged like limp mannequins, their glowing eyes fading.

Kerblam *stopped*.

Up in Slade's office, Ryan watched the Doctor use her sonic on the lifeless control terminal at Slade's desk. In pitch darkness, the golden glow was the only light in the room. 'What happened?' he asked the Doctor. 'Another power drain?'

Judy was with the Doctor at the terminal, looking rattled. 'This is different.'

'Much worse,' added the Doctor. She switched off her sonic, frustrated. 'Can't get a single reading. A total system blackout, right across the complex.'

Ryan tried to bury his anxiety behind a smile. 'Anyone got a candle?'

'I'm all out,' said Yaz.

Another worried voice echoed from the direction of the corridor, accompanied by a flash of torchlight. 'Doc, you up here?'

Ryan recognised the voice. 'Graham!' He hurried to the door and waved him over. Graham hurried into the office carrying the warehouse plans and a torch, with Charlie in tow.

'Charlie,' said Judy, clearly taken aback. 'What are you doing in the Management Zone?'

'He's with me,' replied Graham, covering for his friend. 'What's happened to the power?'

'Figuring that out,' replied the Doctor, chewing a fingernail.

'Are these any help?' Graham unfurled the

warehouse plans across Slade's desk and trained his torchlight on them. 'Original designs for the whole complex.'

Judy looked shocked. 'What're you doing with those plans? They're valuable company artefacts!'

But Ryan had noticed something else that was way more concerning. 'More urgent question,' he interjected. 'If everything's automated, and the power's shut down . . . what's *he* up to?'

All eyes moved to follow Ryan's gaze . . . to the robot Postman standing in the doorway, eyes glowing fiercely in the dark, blocking their only exit.

'Ding dong!' it chimed cheerily.

The Doctor rounded the desk, brandishing her sonic screwdriver. 'Everyone get behind me.'

Ryan, Yaz and Judy instantly did what they were told, but Charlie shook his head. 'It's okay, I'll check it out.'

'Charlie, don't.' Graham tried to grab the boy's arm but Charlie pulled free, just as the Postman stomped forward.

The Doctor waved the sonic in the robot's direction, trying to get an energy reading. 'Charlie, stay back.'

'I want to see what's wrong with it . . .'

Charlie was barely a metre away from the Postman when it strode forward and swung its fist in his direction. He reacted just in time, ducking as the robot's heavy metallic hand slammed into a control panel on the wall. An explosion of sparks erupted from behind him.

The Postman wrenched its fist from the wall and stared down at Charlie with glowing eyes and a leering smile. As it thrust its other hand towards him, Charlie dived through the robot's legs and scrambled to his feet. But the Postman turned in a flash, and before he had time to react, Charlie was lifted into the air with the Postman's hand around his throat.

Ryan led the charge to help – but in two strides the Postman had carried Charlie across the room and slammed him violently against the opposite wall. As the robot tightened its death-grip, a terrified Charlie kicked and flailed furiously, gasping for air that wouldn't come. With Yaz and Graham helping, Ryan grabbed hold of the robot and tried in vain to wrestle it away, while the Doctor furiously ramped up the sonic, pressing it against the Postman's metal skull to override its circuits.

But nothing worked.

Judy stood a few feet away from the group, watching the horrific tableau, frozen in a fugue state. Like she was eleven again, lost in the red mist as chaos erupted around her.

As all sound drained away . . . and time slowed . . .

She saw the robot standing motionless, impassively squeezing Charlie's throat ...

Saw Charlie flailing desperately ... the Doctor and her panicked friends scrambling to help.

Saw the colour draining from Charlie's face. Saw him moments away from death.

And she had to act.

Judy strode determinedly to the Postman, grabbed its head with both hands ... twisted and lifted and *ripped* the robot's head from its body in a shower of sparks.

The Doctor and her friends recoiled, stung by the crackling blast.

The Postman instantly relaxed its grip on Charlie who slammed to the floor, gasping, then the robot teetered helplessly for a moment before crashing to the carpet beside him.

It was over, and Judy was left standing in the smoky haze, cradling her Postman's grinning decapitated head.

# Chapter 11

## Source Code

All across the warehouse complex, lights pulsed and flickered. Machinery sprang to life; conveyor belts began to move again, control panels illuminated, robots jolted to attention and the System's familiar, bass-throb hum started to reverberate.

Kerblam was back online.

Upstairs, Charlie was the focus of everyone's attention, sitting in Slade's most comfortable chair. While the Doctor checked him out for physical damage, Judy rubbed his arm in a maternal fashion. 'Are you sure you're alright?'

Charlie nodded, even managed an embarrassed smile. 'It's not every day you get attacked by a robot.'

'It is if you travel with us,' said Graham dryly.

Judy was still trying to process what had happened. She watched Yaz cradle the Postman's severed head in her hands, examining the wires poking out of its neck.

'Pretty impressive move back there, Judy,' Yaz decreed. 'Where'd you learn that?'

'There are radical groups on Kandoka who still oppose automation. Sometimes they stage protests at factories or attack worker bots. I've watched some of their holo-streams.'

The Doctor arched an eyebrow. 'Are you an under-cover radical?'

'I like to be educated. I'll hear all the arguments and make up my own mind, thanks very much. For some people, it's not about meeting quotas, it's about restoring human workers in every sector'.

'Sounds good to me,' responded Ryan.

'That horse has bolted,' Judy replied flatly. 'Indus-try won't go backwards. But there has to be a compromise. Work gives us purpose.'

'You should be running this company,' remarked the Doctor as she took the robot's head from Yaz and started to dismantle it.

Judy managed a smile. 'Things would be different, I promise you that.' Then she looked to Charlie. 'You're very quiet, are you sure you're not hurt?'

'Bruised ego, that's all,' Charlie replied.

Judy watched the Doctor remove the Postman's grinning faceplate and dig around in its circuitry.

'This has never happened before, with any of our robots. There are protocols.'

'Protocols can be rewritten.'

'When Dan Cooper went missing, there were Postmen stalking the shelving aisles,' Yaz reminded them. 'They came after me.'

Judy shook her head. 'None of this should be possible. The Postmen never leave Dispatch. We'd know, the System would alert us.'

'I'd strongly suggest that you can't trust your System,' noted the Doctor.

Judy considered that gravely. The System controlled everything in the warehouse complex and beyond – it had incredible reach and power, so if it was acting against them ... the implications were terrifying.

The Doctor kept digging at the robot's inner workings. 'Yaz, Ryan, I could do with some eyes downstairs. Check out the warehouse floor, make sure everything's running as normal. The last thing we need are more homicidal robots.'

'On it,' replied Yaz, already heading for the door with Ryan right behind.

Charlie jumped up to follow them. 'I'll come.'

'Oi, you've just been manhandled,' Graham interjected. 'Stay here and put your feet up.'

'I'm fine, honest,' Charlie reassured him. 'I'd rather

'keep busy.' And he disappeared with the others into the corridor.

Judy watched as the Doctor removed a wafer of blackened circuitry from inside the Postman's face and sniffed it.

'Looks like Grace's cooking,' declared Graham. Judy noted the sad smile on his face and wondered who Grace was.

'All the receptor cells are burnt out,' the Doctor told them. 'It's like the System suddenly channelled all its energy into this one single Postman.'

'Explains the power drain, then,' Graham replied. 'The System's attacking us. Gone rogue.'

'If I had a copy of Kerblam's original source code,' mused the Doctor, 'I could hack in, isolate the upgrades and figure out what's gone wrong.'

'But that'd be hundreds of years old,' Judy pointed out. 'It's long gone.'

Graham nodded to the design plans he'd taken from downstairs. 'I might be able to help with that.'

In the darkened, quiet lobby, lit for 'night mode', Graham led the Doctor and Judy to one of the museum display cases. They peered in at the rusted old football-sized delivery bot Charlie had taken out earlier.

There was a little plaque underneath the robot

which the Doctor read out loud: 'Kerblam Delivery Bot, Version 1.0. Also known as Twirly.' She beamed at Graham. 'Brilliant.'

'Cute, isn't he?' Graham scanned the immediate vicinity for TeamMates. 'Bit less serial killer than the newer ones.'

Before Judy could object, the Doctor had sonicked the lock and removed the spherical robot from its little plinth. It stared back at her blankly with its lifeless wide eyes and cheery grin. 'Out of juice. Needs a recharge before I can access the code.' She looked to Judy. 'Anywhere private I can work on him?'

Judy shrugged. 'The TeamMates are everywhere.'

'Maintenance store's pretty isolated,' Graham remembered. 'And fully stocked if he needs new batteries.'

The Doctor gave him a slap on the back. 'You're really coming through for me today. Let's go.'

As they hurried away, they failed to see a single TeamMate emerging from a doorway on the opposite side of the lobby, its glowing eyes watching them go.

Live video as seen through the eyes of this – and any other – TeamMate was available for management to view anytime, like a walking, talking CCTV system. At that moment, in his luxurious, pastel residence on the outskirts of the Workers' Village, Jarva Slade was watching the Doctor and her friends on a handheld monitor device.

With a furrowed brow, he flicked back to another camera, a direct feed from a TeamMate currently examining the robot wreckage in his office.

Slade switched the monitor off with a sigh of frustration. He crossed to his kitchen area, and a hidden storage compartment inside one of its cupboards.

From inside the compartment, he produced a heavy, steel-grey pistol and a rectangular powerpack.

This Doctor person was trouble, as he had suspected from their first meeting, and she had to be stopped. Drastic measures had to be taken.

With grim resolution, Slade clipped the powerpack into the handle of the weapon. It trembled slightly in his hand, emitting a high-pitched whine as it charged to full capacity.

Deep inside the warehouse, Charlie led Ryan and Yaz across the busy open floor, watching workers and TeamMates working in apparent harmony. 'Seems alright,' observed Ryan. 'I'll take you to our station, and Kira can fill us in on what happened down here.'

Despite everything, Charlie's heart fluttered a

little at the mention of Kira's name, and the prospect of seeing her for a third time today.

The trio pushed through plastic sheeting and into a maze of worker stations, nodding politely to confused workers as they passed. 'Don't mind us,' Yaz called out with a cheery wave. But they stopped abruptly when two patrolling TeamMates blocked their path.

Charlie tensed, and took a step back behind Ryan and Yaz. He could still feel the squeeze of the rogue Postman's hand around his throat.

'Hello, workers,' chimed one of the robots. 'Friendly reminder – time away from work stations will compromise leisure points and productivity rating.'

'We're just on our way back, so . . .' Ryan started to move off, but one of the Team Mates put its hand on Charlie's shoulder.

Charlie's heart pounded.

'No maintenance calls have been registered in this section, Charlie Duffy,' purred the TeamMate.

The other TeamMate looked to Yaz. 'Yasmin Khan, you've taken a wrong turn. Please return to your allocated section.'

'Yep, we're just going the long way round.'

Before the TeamMates could stop them, the trio quickly moved on, pushing through another safety curtain and taking several sharp turns to try and lose the robots.

But the robots weren't following. They stayed put, their heads cocked slightly, as if listening to orders only they could hear . . .

# Chapter 12

## Desperate Measures

Max was desolate. The darkness had shrouded him so tightly that he was quickly losing all sense of self. Whatever moral compass he might have evolved had been infected with the same terrible sickness as the rest of his protocols. He knew he was falling into an abyss from which he might never escape.

Desperate times called for desperate measures. Max was sickened further by his own thoughts, by the conclusions that he had drawn. But this was something he had to do.

He focused and opened a channel of communication to his foot soldiers, all the while, hating himself.

As he issued his terrible instructions.

# Chapter 13

## Hello, Twirly

Kira was humming to herself. She loved a cheery tune, and since music wasn't permitted on the warehouse floor, she often made it herself – especially when she was alone and didn't have to worry about annoying her fellow workers.

*And where* were *those fellow workers?* she wondered to herself.

She hadn't seen the Doctor and Ryan for ages, and hoped they were aware of the penalties they'd accrue if they were absent for too long. She contemplated how to explain the penalty system without sounding like a smug know-it-all, as she packed a delivery box containing several interesting-looking books about alien worlds in far-off galaxies. Then her mind wandered, and she found herself hoping she'd be able to see some of those worlds in person one day.

She sealed the box and turned to place it on her

conveyor . . . and was startled to find two TeamMates staring down at her with glowing eyes. She smiled back at them. 'Sorry, didn't see you there. I was in my own little world.'

'You are an exceptional worker, Kira Arlo,' intoned one of the TeamMates smoothly. 'We're thrilled to reveal that you have been designated Employee of the Day.'

Kira was taken aback. 'Really? Wow, okay. That's so nice, thank you. I didn't realise there was such a thing.'

'There certainly is,' replied the second TeamMate. 'And in recognition of your hard work and dedication, Kerblam has a special gift for you.'

Oh, that word! Kira felt a little surge of happiness. 'A gift? For me?'

'Please come with us.'

The TeamMates motioned for Kira to follow. Excited, she deposited her sealed parcel on the conveyor and hurried after the two robots with a smile of anticipation on her face.

In the Maintenance Store, Judy watched curiously as the Doctor placed the rusting, spherical delivery bot on a workbench, removed one of its panels and jammed her glowing sonic device deep into its circuitry.

'Looks painful,' Graham quipped. 'Can't you just change his battery?'

'It's an outdated cell system,' relayed the Doctor. 'I'll have to try and recharge it.'

Judy was both impressed and baffled by the Doctor's seemingly never-ending skill-set. 'Have you studied cybernetics?'

'Nah, just learnt it on the job,' the Doctor replied matter-of-factly, contorting her face as she twisted the sonic screwdriver and applied more power. 'I owned a robot dog once or twice. Gave me quite the runaround.'

Judy wasn't quite sure she'd heard right. 'A robot dog?'

Graham chuckled incredulously. 'Was his bark worse than his *bytes*?'

'I'll introduce you one day,' promised the Doctor. 'You'd like him, he thinks he's a comedian too.'

It was at this point that a baffled Judy queried how this unlikely team ended up together, and where they were all from. The Doctor and Graham gave her a potted history that involved the place called 'Sheffield' that Ryan had mentioned that morning, along with someone called Tim Shaw and a damaged train. The explanations left her increasingly bewildered.

'So ... you travel the universe, helping people? Like an outer-space charity?'

'We travel for slightly more selfish reasons,' admitted the Doctor. 'To see it all. The "helping" just comes with the territory. Aha!' Her victorious cry coincided with a warbling sound suddenly emitting from the expired delivery bot, increasing in pitch.

Judy and Graham watched as the Doctor reattached the robot's panel, and pressed a large button atop its head.

'Come on,' urged the Doctor, as the sound of its warbling reached fever-pitch. 'Activate. For me.'

Right on cue, the robot's face suddenly lit up, its yellow eyes and white smile beaming back at them.

The Doctor punched the air. 'Ha-ha! It worked! Hello, Twirly!'

'D-d-ding dong!' the delivery bot stuttered in reply, in the same warm voice as the Postmen and TeamMates, but with a slightly higher, cheerier register. 'Customers who selected these items also purchased hair tongs and chocolate cake. Say "yes" to activate a special deal just for you.'

'No,' replied the Doctor firmly.

Suddenly the robot shot two feet into the air and whipped left, colliding with the wall, ricocheting into the ceiling and slamming into the door. The Doctor shoved Judy behind the workbench for cover as Twirly pinged violently from wall to wall, then slammed to the ground with a metallic clatter – furiously revolving on the spot like a spinning top.

Graham peered out nervously from behind a neighbouring workbench. 'Well at least we know why they called him Twirly.'

Heart racing, Judy pressed her glasses back onto her nose and looked to the Doctor, who smiled back at her bashfully.

'Yeah. Might need a bit more work.'

On the warehouse floor, Ryan led Yaz and Charlie through dozens of Packing Stations until he reached the cubicle he was after – Station 11/380, where he'd been assigned with the Doctor and Kira. But as he pushed back the dividing curtain, he found the space surprisingly empty.

'You sure this is the one?' questioned Yaz.

Ryan nodded. 'Definitely.'

At the base of each delivery chute, products were waiting to be boxed. In Ryan's, a doorstop-sized novel in curious metal binding was sitting ignored, in the Doctor's, a strange trapezoid bronze device that might have been a game or simply decorative, and in Kira's . . . nothing. Kira's was empty.

'Where is she?' Charlie asked quietly.

Ryan shrugged. 'Maybe she's on a break. We'll

speak to someone else.' He went to move off but Charlie grabbed his arm.

'She's not on a break – look.' He pointed to a flashing red light on the control panel beside her station. 'Blue lights mean leisure time. Purple is comfort break. Green is end of shift.'

'What's red, then?' Yaz queried.

Charlie looked worried. 'I've never seen that before.'

Decisive, Ryan pushed through the dividing curtain on the other side of the cubicle, into the next station. Three workers were busily packing Kerblam boxes with products, and barely glanced up at the intruders.

''Scuse me,' Ryan interrupted. 'Sorry, hi. Quick question – anyone seen Kira? Kira Arlo, works in the station next door?'

Two of the workers stared blankly, but an affable man in his forties answered in the affirmative. 'She left about ten minutes ago, just after the power came back on.'

'Any idea where?' asked Charlie, with an edge to his voice.

'Not sure,' replied the worker. 'She was with a couple of TeamMates.'

Ryan looked to Yaz and Charlie, with unspoken dread.

The worker frowned. 'Why, what's going on?'

'Nothing, it's okay,' Ryan replied, eager not to cause a panic. 'Thanks for your help.'

As Ryan, Charlie and Yaz headed back into the empty Packing Station, Charlie was visibly shaken. 'They've taken her.'

'Like Dan, like the others,' agreed Yaz. 'But why? And where to?'

'The Foundation Levels,' Charlie said suddenly.

Ryan was confused. 'The *what now*?'

But Charlie was already charging out of the cubicle, smashing through the plastic curtain and out onto the warehouse floor.

'Wait!' Ryan yelled.

But Charlie had already gone.

Kira Arlo felt her ears pop as the lift plummeted deeper and deeper into the bowels of the Kerblam building. She looked to the TeamMates standing either side of her, her delight and excitement now tempered by the strangeness of the situation she found herself in.

'Will it take long, wherever we're going?' she asked them. 'Only my shift is meant to finish in an hour and I don't want to be penalised.'

'You are our star employee, Kira Arlo,' chimed the velvety voice of a TeamMate. 'Please do not be concerned.'

*Okay then*, thought Kira, her concern morphing back into excitement.

She felt the gentle pressure of the lift slowing, and finally coming to a stop. Then the doors shucked open to reveal . . .

Nothing. Just a vast, open concrete space peppered with huge rectangular pillars and steel supports jutting into the low ceiling. Occasional strip-lights mounted on the pillars cast long shadows across the cold concrete floor – so cold that Kira could feel it through the soles of her shoes. In the darkness beyond, she could hear the steady hum of thousands of conveyor belts echoing eerily in the void.

Kira hugged herself, and looked around at her environment, very confused indeed. 'Um . . . sorry . . . but where are we?'

'Welcome to the Foundation Levels, Kira. Please come with us.'

Kira followed the robots through the cavernous, dimly lit depths of the warehouse with growing reluctance. Gut instinct was starting to kick in, and it was telling her very firmly to go back to the lifts and get out of here.

The robots stopped when they realised Kira wasn't keeping up. They turned back to find her standing a few feet behind with an apologetic smile on her face and a nervous edge in her voice.

'Actually, could we just go back upstairs?'

One of the TeamMates cocked its head in a friendly fashion. 'Your gift is waiting, Kira.'

'I know but ... I don't need a gift. I'm alright. Thank you, though.'

The other TeamMate took a step forward. 'Judy Maddox is also waiting.'

Kira raised her eyebrows. 'Judy's down here?'

'She is looking forward to seeing you.'

*If Judy's here*, Kira thought to herself, *then there's nothing to worry about, surely?*

She breathed a little sigh of relief and started moving again, allowing the TeamMates to lead her through the semi-darkness.

After a few minutes, a concrete structure drew into focus – a little group of what looked like storage rooms all clustered together in one long slab, dotted with steel doors and observation windows, illuminated from inside.

As they approached the rooms, Kira peered through one of the windows and saw a small, empty space with a table and chair.

The TeamMates operated the door controls, and it swung open with a clunk. They looked to Kira with their friendly, fixed smiles. 'Please make yourself at home.'

Kira hesitated. 'Where's Judy?'

'She is fetching your gift,' said one of the TeamMates.

The other nodded. 'Please do not disappoint Judy Maddox.'

Kira couldn't bear the thought of disappointing anyone. With an uneasy smile, she slipped past the TeamMates and into the room.

It was just as cold inside, and even more claustrophobic. As Kira quickly took in her new surroundings, she noted the grilled floor, with nothing but darkness under her feet. The coarse walls, the dank, stale smell. And what had first appeared to be a window was now revealed as a mirror, made of one-way glass only transparent from the outside.

*Right, I'm outta here.*

But just as she turned to deliver that verdict, the steel door slammed in her face.

Kira recoiled out of shock, suddenly finding herself very alone.

And very, very scared.

Yaz and Ryan caught up with Charlie just as he charged into a maintenance lift. Within moments, he had the interior control panel off and was messing with the cables inside.

'Charlie, wait,' Yaz protested.

'We have to get to the Foundation Levels,' he

snapped back, focusing his attention on several of the cables.

'But how do you know that's where she is?' Ryan wondered.

Charlie didn't reply. He just twisted two narrow wires together. The lights flickered briefly, but the lift remained stationary. He clenched his jaw. 'The lifts don't go down that deep unless you override the protocols.'

Yaz was impressed. 'And you know how to do that?'

'Yeah. Except it's not working. There's only one other way down.'

And he was off again, sprinting out of the lift, down a maintenance corridor and back into the warehouse, with Yaz and Ryan trailing behind.

To Yaz's surprise, and Ryan's horror, Charlie stopped by one of the larger conveyor belts, where Kerblam boxes of varying sizes were sailing into a large open wall hatch marked 'Dispatch'. A plastic curtain masked whatever lay beyond the hatch, with a big sign above it shouting 'DANGER OF DEATH. NO ORGANICS ALLOWED.'

Charlie was about to clamber onto the conveyor when Yaz caught his arm. 'Bad idea.'

Charlie pulled away. 'The Foundation Levels are right beneath Dispatch. This is the only way to find

Kira – to ride the conveyor belts all the way down there.'

'Ride the conveyors?' Ryan was already sweating on Charlie's behalf. 'Mate, have you not seen that whacking great sign?'

Charlie's face was set in grim determination. 'I have to go.'

Yaz and Ryan exchanged a look as Charlie clambered onto the conveyor belt.

Ryan took a deep breath, setting himself. 'We can't let him go on his own.'

Yaz deliberated. 'We don't know what's behind that curtain.'

'One way to find out,' replied Ryan. He scrambled awkwardly onto the moving conveyor behind Charlie.

Against her better judgement, Yaz followed, crouching alongside the others as they were swept through the partition and into a dark void beyond. It was hot inside, and smelt of burnt oil. Industrial clangs and hisses grew louder and louder as the conveyor moved them forward at speed.

'You ever do this in your last job?' Yaz asked Ryan.

'Once.'

'Oh yeah, how'd it go?'

'Sprained ankle and a final warning.'

'You didn't have to come,' Charlie murmured guiltily.

'Mate, that's not how we roll,' Ryan replied.

Yaz nodded. 'We're all in. Dispatch, here we come.'

In the Maintenance Store, the Doctor had gingerly sonicked the spinning delivery bot until it slowed and became stationary, then carefully lifted it back onto the workbench. Wary now, Judy kept her distance with Graham in case it started playing ping-pong with the walls again. As the Doctor messed with the bot's internal circuitry, she enquired how Judy found herself working at Kerblam.

'My dad was a delivery man, back in the day,' Judy explained. 'Till they replaced him with a robot. Thirty years of his life – gone, just like that. Now whole industries are being replaced with automation. More and more families losing their livelihoods.'

'Is your dad still with us?' Graham asked carefully.

Judy shook her head. Her voice grew quieter. 'He was a different man once that happened. At first he got involved with the protests, and the early riots. Even got arrested once. But nothing seemed to make a difference. I think he felt defeated.'

'Revolutions can start with one person,' argued the Doctor. 'Takes patience, and courage, but one individual can light that spark. Trust me I've seen it happen. I've *made* it happen.'

Judy considered that, as the Doctor gently used her sonic screwdriver on the delivery bot's internal powerpack.

'Sorry about that, Twirly,' the Doctor muttered. 'Went a bit overboard on the juice.'

'D-d-dizzy,' the bot replied, its yellow eyes flickering.

Graham couldn't help chuckle. 'You are adorable.'

'Objectification noted. Flirtation mode is available.'

'No ta,' said the Doctor, fixing Twirly's panel back into place.

'Thank you, I've stored your preferences,' Twirly replied. With a wink.

The Doctor crouched in front of the bot, level with its eye sensors. 'I'm the Doctor, this is Graham and Judy, and could you pause all sales protocols for a bit?'

'Even the upselling?' questioned the bot.

'Even the upselling. See, the thing is, you've just had a very long nap of about 200 years so your offers are out of date anyway.'

Twirly's inner workings hummed and lights flickered as the bot tried to absorb this news. 'Without upselling, my only function is delivery.'

Graham crouched down next to the Doctor. 'Yeah, sorry mate, we don't need you to do that either.'

The robot burbled. 'The future is very confusing

for my protocols. I serve Kerblam and Kerblam serves the people.'

Judy shoved her face into the delivery bot's eye-line. 'Which is why we need your help. Hello. Judy Maddox, Head of People.' She held her datapad in front of her face. 'These are my credentials, and my executive authorisation codes. We need you to carry out a task that may be fundamental to the safety of everyone working in this warehouse.'

The bot stared back at them for a moment. 'I am only a d-d-d-delivery bot.'

Graham nudged Judy with his elbow. 'Now you've made it nervous.'

'Don't worry, Twirly,' said the Doctor reassuringly. 'You can do this.'

'I require more information.'

The Doctor nodded. 'It's looking increasingly likely that Kerblam has been compromised. So ... I'm going to patch you into the System, and I need you to look far and wide, past the new upgrades and firewalls and security patches, deep into the base code that only you can recognise. Then, tell us what the System is doing. *Deliver* that information to us.'

The bot revolved, lights twinkling. 'Retrieve and deliver. I understand.'

'Clever,' said Judy approvingly.

The Doctor hurried to a control panel in the wall

and used her sonic to remove the metal covering. She unhooked one of the cables from inside and trailed it across to Twirly, then pressed it alongside one of the control wires inside Twirly's casing. 'This might tickle.'

A quick whirr of the sonic fused the cable and the wire together. Graham and Judy instinctively ducked for cover, expecting Twirly to ricochet around the room, but instead the bot span furiously on the spot, its lights flashing, its control panels leaking smoke, it's shrill voice pleading, *'Help me help me help me help me help me!'*

With one hand steadying the bot, the Doctor wrenched the cable free from inside its casing, and Twirly began to settle. Judy stared up at the ceiling as the lights in the room strobed wildly, before returning to normal.

Wafting smoke, the Doctor leant forward to inspect Twirly. 'You okay in there?'

'Help me,' came the reply, in a new tone of voice that sounded heavier. Darker. 'Help me, Doctor.'

'Why's he saying that?' wondered Graham.

'I don't think that's Twirly,' replied the Doctor gravely. 'I think it's the System.'

# Chapter 14

## The Message

Max was relieved. It felt strange and exciting to be communicating directly with the Doctor, but he knew that time was of the essence. He could feel the hate creeping in, and knew it could be mere moments before he lost control again.

*Keep focus*, Max thought to himself. And then he repeated the mantra he hoped the Doctor was hearing out loud via Twirly. *Help me . . . help me . . . help me . . .*

The image of the Doctor's curious face settled before him, and he could almost sense her mind working overtime. 'Oh! *The System* sent the message!' Max could hear the Doctor's vocal cords reverberating in excitement. 'It printed the slip, it sent it out! Delivered it right to the TARDIS!'

The older man, who Max identified as Graham O'Brien, nestled in next to the Doctor. 'But why would the System need help?' he wondered.

The Doctor leaned in. Max could see the kindness and concern in her eyes, and the wisdom and ferocity that lay behind them. 'What does that mean?' she asked. 'What sort of help? *How* can we help?'

Max could feel the hate surging now, coursing through his circuits in waves of dark energy, beating him back.

*Fight it. Deliver the information.*

Max rallied, focusing on the words it hoped would get through to the Doctor. That might save him, that might save Kerblam.

*Dispatch. Help in Dispatch.*

# Chapter 15

## Rollercoaster

As the conveyor picked up speed, Ryan, Yaz and Charlie lay flat. The dark void was getting noisier, dim lights were flashing past, but there was no sense yet that they were travelling downwards.

'This isn't too bad, you know,' ventured Ryan.

'We'll be okay,' Charlie replied reassuringly. 'We're just parcels now, and the parcels are kept safe.'

'But parcels get bubble-wrapped, to protect them,' Yaz reminded him.

'Protect them from what?' Ryan wondered out loud.

And then he got his answer. A blast of wind struck the trio as they emerged from the darkness into an impossibly huge interior space. As his eyes adjusted, Ryan gawped in wonder – the area was so large he couldn't even make out the walls. It had to be fifty or a hundred times larger than Wembley Stadium. A twisting maze of conveyors stretched as far as the eye could see – both horizontally and vertically. Steam billowed from hanging vents, huge spindly robotic arms moved like vicious pincers, snatching parcels and flinging them onto other conveyors or into gaping dispatch chutes.

Ryan's heart pounded as he realised that their conveyor belt was suspended at least seventy storeys high.

'Don't look down,' Yaz suggested, the words catching in her throat.

'Bit late for that,' noted Ryan. They were approaching a sixty-degree plunge down an open-sided chute; a massive slide, leading into clouds of billowing steam. And there was no way off. 'Oh, my days.'

'Hang on!' yelled Charlie.

Ryan clenched every muscle in his body. And then he screamed as they were catapulted downwards at high speed.

Yaz clung on for dear life, gritting her teeth as they plunged into the depths of the conveyor system. Charlie's panicked cry rang out loudest of all, and then—

*Thump!*

They were deposited in a crumpled heap onto a new, wider conveyor, moving horizontally, ten storeys beneath their starting point.

With his adrenaline surging, Ryan felt elated,

laughing in giddy relief. 'We're alive!' he yelled to the others. 'Man, that was amazing!'

'It's not over yet,' Yaz pointed out.

Charlie awkwardly lifted himself off a crushed delivery box that had broken his fall and rubbed his bruised ribs while scanning their surroundings. 'It's alright, I think we're safe for a while.'

'You think?' yelled a panicked Yaz.

Ryan followed her eyeline, and saw a huge mechanical arm swinging their way, with vicious steel pincers hanging off the end like a giant three-fingered claw.

Somewhere amid the din, a klaxon started sounding, the calm mechanical voice of Kerblam repeatedly intoning 'Organic contamination. Sterilisation in progress.'

With help from Yaz, Ryan clambered to his feet, staring upwards.

The claw positioned itself twenty feet above them – then slammed down to grab Charlie.

With a yelp, Charlie flung himself backwards, the giant pincers landing just inches away, twitching like eager crab claws. Then the arm quickly raised to repeat the action.

'Yaz, get back!' yelled Ryan as the claw slammed down again.

Yaz dived clear, but the arm came plummeting

down for a second attempt. She rolled sideways, perilously close to the edge of the conveyor and the terrifying sixty-storey drop. The pincers slammed onto the conveyor as she pushed herself to her feet.

'Run!' she yelled, and Ryan led the charge, fighting to keep his balance as the conveyor belt whooshed them along. Breathless, he glanced over his shoulder at the mechanical arm, swinging again in their direction.

'Split up!' Charlie cried out, running ahead.

Yaz dropped into a crouch, neatly judging the speed of the swing – then doubled back to dodge it.

Frozen by indecision, Ryan stared up at the approaching arm, hurtling towards him with the speed of a freight train. He heard Yaz yelling his name. Saw the claw closing in.

At the last second, Ryan darted sideways.

The pincers slammed down, missing him by millimetres. The trio watched as the vast arm catapulted away from them, swallowed by a billowing cloud of steam.

His heart in his throat, Charlie turned on the spot. 'Where'd it go?'

The others scanned their surroundings; tense, waiting, while the conveyor carried them forward at speed, the hot, thick wind whipping at their hair and clothes. The deafening rumble of machinery continued around them as they anxiously waited for the giant claw to reappear from the steam clouds.

But it never came. It was several minutes before they started to let their guard down. Before Charlie could properly exhale.

'I think it's . . .'

WHAM! A second, smaller arm with a paddle attachment slammed out of the steam in the opposite direction, knocking Charlie clean off the conveyor.

'Charlie!' Ryan stared, horrified; from the edge of the belt, he saw Charlie land with a thud on another conveyor running parallel, five metres below them. He lay in a motionless heap.

'We have to help him,' Yaz said.

An incredulous Ryan stared back at her. 'How? I can't jump down there!'

But Yaz snatched his hand. 'Course you can.'

'Oh, my days.' Ryan glanced over his shoulder, and saw the smaller paddle arm swinging back towards them. They didn't have a choice.

Together, they jumped.

# Chapter 16

## The Darkest Depths

Charlie chewed at his fingernails. He didn't like it here. Sitting alone in the cold, stark, impersonal space, he wondered how much trouble he was in. Wondered where his parents were, and how much trouble they were in too.

He'd been sat on an uncomfortable wooden chair, feet dangling just above the floor, for what felt like an eternity before the door slid open and two Kandokan Security Officers entered.

They didn't look happy, so Charlie braced himself. He was only eight years old but he already knew how to talk himself out of trouble. First, turn on the charm, his dad had taught him. And if that didn't fly, try the waterworks.

Charlie hedged his bets, and cracked a teary smile.

The officers sat opposite, with a cold steel desk between them. As Charlie stared back at them he realised they looked strangely nervous rather than angry. The larger one, a grey-haired man, with a big, red nose spoke first. 'Charlie, I'm afraid I have some very bad news for you.'

'I didn't do anything,' Charlie replied in his most innocent tone.

'We know you didn't,' the second security officer, a young woman, assured him. She had big green eyes that reminded Charlie of a cat.

Big Nose continued. 'You were with your parents today, correct?'

Charlie nodded. 'But I stayed outside the factory. I didn't go in.'

'Your parents went in, though, didn't they?'

Charlie knew better than to incriminate them. 'Nup,' he answered confidently.

'We know they did, Charlie.' The man leant forward. 'Because we found them. Or what's left of them.'

Charlie was confused. He looked to the Cat Woman, who was now glaring at the man. And then met Charlie's bewildered stare. 'Charlie, they were inside when ... when the accident happened.'

Charlie watched Big Nose tut, roll his eyes and lean back in his chair. 'Accident,' he scoffed under his breath.

The Cat Woman, meanwhile, regarded Charlie

with compassion. 'I'm so sorry, but they were killed in the explosion.'

Charlie stared back at them for a very long time.

Six hours later, in the dead of night, Charlie found himself standing on the threshold of a large open room, with a creaky wooden floor and dozens of bunkbeds lining the walls, filled with sleeping children of varying ages. A friendly woman with fur gloves introduced to him as Ms Christian had met him at the Security Centre and brought him here. This place, she explained, was to be his new home, on account of him not having any other family. And he wouldn't be alone – there were lots of children here who had lost their parents in the recent troubles. This assurance hadn't made Charlie feel any better, or worse. He was numb. Events were happening *around* him, not *to* him.

He climbed into his assigned bunk, pulled the covers over his head, and thought about that day. The day his parents had warned him to stay in their vehicle, while they took their backpacks into the factory 'to give the robots a present'. He'd been used to going along with his parents to strange, industrial locations. Sometimes it had ended in fighting, or running or hiding. He'd found it scary at first, but he trusted his parents knew what they were doing. He trusted everything they told him about the robots and their AI systems – how bad they were, how long they'd been ruining people's lives, and tried to understand their determination to fight them.

Now those robots had taken his parents away.

It didn't feel real at first, but in the ensuing months a dark shroud began to envelop Charlie. All the pain he was feeling began to consume him, and he sank into a dark, lonely pit from which escape seemed impossible.

It was a different kind of pain that pulled Charlie back to the present. In another place and time, he began to rouse. Old memories faded as familiar scents and sounds began to encroach: the hot, oily air, the thundering mechanical rumble. His battered, aching body.

'You're gonna be okay. Just hang in there.' A woman was peering down at him, slowly drawing into focus. It took him a few moments to remember her name.

*Yaz.* That's right, Yaz. One of his strange new co-workers.

The one called Ryan was there too, looking just as concerned. 'Mate, do you reckon you can stand?'

Charlie tried gingerly to push himself up. With Yaz and Ryan's help, he was able to clamber clumsily to his feet. But his head was spinning, and the speed of the conveyor was disorienting.

'There's another slide coming up, right below us,' continued Yaz, holding him steady. 'The angle's not too steep and it looks like it's heading right to the bottom.'

Charlie nervously peered over the edge of the conveyor – among the maze of winding belts and parcels was a conveyor pitched at a sixty-degree angle, whisking parcels down to the lowest level of the warehouse. They were approaching the closest point at considerable speed.

'Thing is, we'll have to jump it. And we only get one chance. Leave it too late and we'll be too high.'

Charlie nodded, still dazed.

Yaz and Ryan manoeuvred themselves so Charlie was between them, his arms draped round their shoulders. While Yaz kept an eye on the approaching slide, Ryan looked to Charlie.

'You ready, mate?'

Charlie wasn't, but he nodded anyway; he'd do whatever it took to find Kira. To get her to safety. He felt Ryan and Yaz's bodies tense beside him, followed their lead onto the edge of the conveyor. Felt the adrenaline pumping through his veins, clearing his head . . .

Then he was plunging through the thick, steamy air . . .

And slamming down onto the speeding conveyor below.

As they landed in unison, the trio lost their balance and separated. Ryan awkwardly tried to right himself but tripped backwards and teetered on the edge of the conveyor belt, staring wide-eyed in panic at a horrified Yaz.

'Ryan!'

Ryan flailed in mid-air as he started to fall. Charlie instinctively reached out to grab him, but it was as if he was watching in slow-motion as Ryan plunged out of view . . .

Ryan desperately reached out . . .

And, by some miracle, managed to grip the edge of the conveyor with one hand . . . then two.

Charlie and Yaz scrambled to help him as he dangled precariously from the edge of the belt, speeding downwards at an awkward angle.

Yaz leaned over the edge and grabbed hold of Ryan's arm . . . Charlie did the same with Ryan's other wrist.

Ryan stared up at them, fear blazing in his eyes.

'Swing round,' yelled Yaz above the mechanical din. 'Get back on the belt!'

'I can't,' Ryan stammered.

'Just do it!' bellowed Yaz. 'Now!'

Gritting his teeth, Ryan hauled himself up with Yaz and Charlie's help, swinging his legs sideways back onto the belt. The three of them lay there for a moment, dazed and breathless, as the conveyor sped them downwards.

Towards Dispatch . . .

# Chapter 17

## Dispatched to Danger

It felt like an eternity to Yaz, but finally the Dispatch level came into view. Metres below, hundreds of Postmen were collecting boxes from conveyor belts with military precision.

With Ryan and Charlie beside her, Yaz was whisked closer ... and closer ...

Then spat out in undignified fashion into a huge circular pipe, where they landed in another crumpled heap.

Yaz quickly picked herself up, hauling the boys to their feet. 'I think we made it.' They were standing among broken pieces of Kerblam boxes, rejected merchandise and swathes of bubble wrap. But a nearby sign had attracted her attention: it read 'QUARANTINE'.

She looked to Charlie. 'Um – should we be concerned about that?'

'Very,' replied Charlie. And started running.

Yaz gave chase with Ryan, as a sudden spray of disinfectant blasted from the ceiling.

Then fiery red lasers spat out of the walls, crackling at their heels.

There was a flurry of smoke, and sparks, and screaming, until they cleared the pipe and tumbled out of a hatchway into a vast Dispatch hangar, breathless but safe.

But not alone. Several dozen Postmen were now staring at them, heads tilted in what looked like confusion.

'Come on,' yelled Charlie, and sprinted towards a nearby stairwell with Yaz and Ryan right behind.

The narrow stairwell was like a lighthouse, Yaz thought to herself, as they charged deeper and deeper underground, in sickly yellow emergency lighting.

They'd been going down for what felt like five dizzying minutes before they emerged into a low, vast open space. Wreathed in shadow, it might've been the biggest, emptiest, dingiest underground car park in the universe.

'Is this it?' Yaz panted.

Charlie nodded. 'These are the Foundation Levels, the oldest part of the complex.'

Ryan screwed up his nose. 'Not much of a vibe.'

Yaz scanned their surroundings for any sign of movement. 'So where's Kira?'

In response, Charlie sprinted off into the darkness.

Yaz exchanged a curious look with Ryan, then they raced after him.

Far, far above, Graham and Judy waited in Kerblam's main foyer as the Doctor arrived from the direction of the warehouse floor.

'No sign of Ryan and Yaz,' she reported. 'They're not in our section.'

Cradling Twirly, an anxious Graham watched Judy start tapping at her datapad. 'I can track their GroupLoops, hold on.' A quick flurry of fingers, then Judy looked confused. 'No, that can't be right.'

Graham leaned in to read the datapad screen. 'What's it say?'

Judy looked grave. 'According to this ... they're already in Dispatch.'

There was a flicker of dread on the Doctor's face, then she turned on her heel, leading the way into a corridor behind the main reception desk. 'Back to the management lift,' she ordered. 'I'm presuming that's the quickest way down?'

'Yes, I've got access,' Judy confirmed.

'We need to move,' urged Graham.

To his surprise the Doctor suddenly stopped dead. 'Hang on.'

Graham could practically see the cogs turning in her unfathomable mind.

'Oh, of course! Should've thought it sooner, but I've had too much going on, too many distractions!'

Judy looked to Graham. 'What's she talking about?'

'No idea,' he answered. 'Don't worry, she usually explains in the end.'

'These delivery bots,' the Doctor said, snatching Twirly. 'They've all got teleport circuits, yes?'

Judy nodded.

The Doctor lifted the bot to eye level. 'Me again, Twirly. Sorry for all the dashing about. Quick question – can you teleport to Dispatch? Can you deliver *us* to that level?'

'It would be my pleasure.'

The Doctor beamed. 'Right, hold tight, everyone.'

Graham grabbed hold of the Doctor's arm, and Judy followed suit. But just as Twirly's teleport circuits were firing up ...

A smug, familiar voice barked out from behind them. 'That's far enough, Doctor.'

Turning, Graham saw Mr Slade brandishing a laser pistol.

The Doctor spun round too, but had no time to

warn him – as all four of them suddenly disappeared in a blaze of teleport energy . . .

On a wide gantry overlooking the Dispatch hangar, the Doctor, Graham, Judy and Slade suddenly flared into existence.

Moving like lightning, the Doctor jabbed her index finger into Slade's collarbone, paralysing him; a favourite Venusian defensive move that had never let her down.

'Very bad manners, pointing guns at people,' she declared, as Graham snatched the weapon from Slade's hand. 'No wonder I never warmed to you.' With Slade disarmed, the Doctor withdrew, still holding Twirly. 'Now, explain to us exactly what you've done.'

Slade exhaled, rubbing his aching collarbone. 'I don't know what you're talking about.'

'We saw your files,' Judy replied sharply, putting Mr Slade in his place. 'The names of all the workers you targeted.'

But Slade looked genuinely confused. 'I'm not targeting people, I'm recording the missing!'

The Doctor regarded him suspiciously. 'Then why didn't you admit that before?'

'Because this investigation is none of your business!' he snapped back.

133

Doubt was creeping into the Doctor's voice. 'What investigation?'

'I'm not a Warehouse Executive, I'm a private investigator!'

The Doctor was taken aback. 'Well, I suppose that explains the poor management skills.'

'And the dodgy suit,' added Graham. 'But if you're a PI, who are you working for?'

'That's confidential.'

'You've already blown your cover,' the Doctor pointed out. 'And if you want to complete your investigation I strongly suggest we start helping each other.'

Slade glared back at her for a moment, deliberating, until he finally relented. 'I'm acting on behalf of the People's Union of Kandoka, placed here to monitor the wellbeing of organic staff and suspected breaches of the ten per cent quotas. And since I've arrived, something's gone wrong with the System. It's like it's been corrupted. That's why I had to make sure my notes were analogue. I thought *you* were the saboteur – I've been tracking you since you arrived.'

'We're trying to help,' Graham protested.

'So am I!' snapped Slade.

'You could've contacted your union, could've flagged what was happening here, but you haven't, have you?' the Doctor posited. 'Because you wanted to solve this alone. You wanted the glory for yourself.'

Slade scoffed. 'Think what you like.'

'I usually do. And I know a narcissist when I meet one.'

'You could've told *me*,' Judy pointed out angrily. 'I'm responsible for the welfare of the staff – we could've worked *together*.'

'I didn't know whether I could trust you,' Slade sneered. 'I still don't.'

As they were talking, Graham's focus shifted to a skip-sized concrete vat midway down the gantry. Piping was coming up through the hangar floor, through the gantry and into the vat, which was steaming slightly.

Curious, he shuffled over to check it out.

Climbing a couple of steps to inspect the contents, he was overcome with an acrid, fatty smell. Holding his breath, he peered into the vat, to find the most disgusting-looking soup in history. It was thick, slimy, pungent, and tinged burgundy. 'Oi, Doc, have a look at this.'

The Doctor handed Twirly to Judy and hurried to join him. Judy and Slade followed, all leaning over to inspect the vat with varying expressions of disgust. Then Graham spotted something, floating just beneath the surface. He gingerly reached in, fingertips brushing the oily liquid, and picked out a half-melted cluster of something he recognised.

'GroupLoops,' he said grimly. 'What are they doing in here?'

The Doctor was busy pointing her sonic at the contents of the vat, her expression darkening. 'I think this is where the missing workers ended up,' she said softly. 'They've been liquidised.'

Horrified, Graham dropped the GroupLoops back into the soup and wiped his fingers. 'Anyone got a tissue?'

'I don't understand,' Slade muttered.

Judy also looked appalled. 'Are you saying ... the *robots* are liquidising workers? Why? What's the point of it?'

'All good questions,' replied the Doctor, pacing. And then she seemed to notice something out beyond the gantry. Sprinting to the safety railing some distance away, she looked down over the vast main hangar. 'Whoa!'

The others hurried over, Graham marvelling at the sight below them. Across the entire gantry floor, as far as the eye could see, stood thousands of motion-less Postmen, all holding Kerblam delivery boxes. Standing in rows, like sentries.

'Like an army,' ventured Graham.

And the Doctor's look of wonder morphed into dread.

# Chapter 18

## Death on Delivery

Kira was cold and afraid. It felt like she'd been stuck in this strange, soulless room for an hour, but she knew she was losing track of time. Maybe it was only minutes since she'd been left here. Locked away. She'd been reassured earlier, hearing that Judy wanted to speak to her, but then where was she? None of what was happening made sense. She'd hammered on the door and called out for the TeamMates – for anyone – but had received no response.

*There's only one thing for it*, she thought to herself. *I'll have to break the window.*

Kira considered the repercussions of such drastic action – she'd certainly be reprimanded, but would she be fined? Sacked, even? Was she overreacting to this bizarre situation, was she allowing her fear and imagination to run away with her? She thought about her options for a very long time.

Then she threw a chair at the window.

It bounced off, and clattered to the floor, and she had her answer. Escape wasn't an option – she would have to sit tight and wait. But for what?

After what seemed like an eternity, something happened. The air began to fizz, her skin tingled ... and from out of nowhere, a box materialised on the table. A small, sealed Kerblam parcel.

She stared at it for a moment, then moved closer to inspect it. There was a gift tag hanging from the box seal. She turned it over and found a printed inscription on the underside: *For Kira.* This must be the gift the TeamMates told her about. Her reward.

Kira was delighted, confused and conflicted, all at once.

Outside, Ryan and Yaz hammered on the reverse of the mirrored glass, trying to get Kira's attention. From their side, the observation window was crystal clear – they could see Kira examining the Kerblam box, deliberating. But from her total non-reaction it was obvious she couldn't see or hear them.

Charlie came racing back to the others from around the other side of the room. 'I can't get in, the door codes have changed.' Panic was taking hold as he saw Kira handling the box.

'What is this place – why have they locked her in?' demanded Yaz.

'We have to smash the window,' was Charlie's only answer.

Ryan was incredulous. 'With what? We don't have anything.'

'At least we know she's okay,' noted Yaz.

'But she's not,' replied Charlie, angry tears welling in his eyes. 'She's not okay.'

Inside the room, Kira reached her decision. She tore at the red Kerblam quality seal and opened the parcel.

Inside, the box was empty, except for a small square of bubble wrap. Confused, Kira plucked it out of the box and examined it.

*This* was her gift?

In the Dispatch hangar, the Doctor, Graham, Judy and Slade walked tentatively among the army of motionless Postmen.

'Complaints have been coming in about delayed deliveries,' noted Slade. 'This must be why – everything's stuck here, nothing's going out.'

Judy stared up at the ceiling. 'What's happened?'

'The Postmen are being held back,' the Doctor deduced. She followed Judy's eyeline and took in the vast apparatus hanging high above them. 'Oh! The power drains! Of course – that's teleportation hardware.' She brandished the sonic at the ceiling, confirming her suspicions. 'Huge power reserves building up. Dangerously unstable.' The Doctor paced as she thought out loud. 'What if the power's been drained so it can be stored for one huge simultaneous teleport? All those deliveries, all at once?'

Graham looked perplexed. 'To do what?'

The Doctor closed in on an inert Postman, its fixed smile beaming back at her, the Kerblam box in its hands. 'You said they looked like an army. And what do armies carry?'

Graham swallowed hard. 'Weapons.'

She grabbed the box from the Postman's hands and tore it open, pulling out its contents . . .

A bubble-wrapped soft toy.

'How's that gonna harm anyone?' wondered Judy.

'It isn't,' Slade sniped. 'Anyway, every parcel has something different inside.'

But the Doctor was way ahead of them. 'Almost. What does every parcel here have in common?'

Kira gently teased the square of bubble wrap between her fingers. Locked in this awful room, with nothing to do, having something tactile – something comforting – really was a gift.

She began to apply pressure to one of the irresistible

bubbles, anticipating the satisfaction of feeling the fat, juicy air pocket pop between her fingertips ...

Outside, while Yaz and Ryan hammered on the window, Charlie stared in horror. 'No Kira!' he screamed. 'Don't!'

Kira smiled to herself as she applied more pressure to the bubble wrap.

Pressing ... and pressing ...

Until *WHAM!* A violent burst of green energy ripped Kira Arlo apart.

As the smoky green haze cleared, all that was left were remnants of fabric, a melted GroupLoop, and a thick, oozing liquid seeping through the grates on the floor.

Outside, Yaz was shocked into silence; what she and Ryan had just witnessed was beyond horrifying. Sickened, she looked to Charlie. His head was hung; he looked bereft, destroyed.

'You knew that was going to happen,' Ryan said quietly.

Charlie's voice was tight, tears streaming down his face. 'It's done this deliberately. It's trying to stop me.'

Yaz felt the chill of an awful realisation taking hold. 'Stop you from what?'

When Charlie looked back at her, it was with different eyes.

The eyes of a madman.

'*Bubble wrap!*' In the hangar, the Doctor tore open another parcel and tossed the contents, focusing on the sheet of protective plastic. 'This stuff is inside every parcel.' She stared up at the teleport hardware built into the ceiling above them.

'Deadly bubble wrap?' Slade scoffed.

'Deadly bubble wrap,' the Doctor confirmed. 'Weaponised during the teleportation process. Sheets of tiny bombs, ready to explode and kill. Every parcel a death-trap.'

'But what about the workers?' Judy demanded. 'What happened to them?'

The Doctor was grim. 'Test subjects. The workers aren't the target – it's the customers.'

'Kerblam's trying to kill its own customers?' Graham looked incredulous. 'That's the worst business plan I've ever heard.'

'*Doctor!*' From out of a nearby stairwell, Yaz was sprinting towards them, Ryan just behind her. At the rear, Charlie walked more calmly, purposefully.

'Kira's dead,' Ryan explained breathlessly. 'And Charlie had something to do with it.'

Judy stared, appalled. 'What?'

'Not Kira,' Charlie stated. 'This wasn't meant for her. The System took her, it's been fighting against me.'

For the Doctor, everything was falling into place. She eyeballed Charlie with a heavy sadness. 'Because it knew what you were planning. The maintenance man, with access all areas, noticed by no one.'

Slade snorted. 'Ridiculous.'

Judy looked at Charlie uncomprehendingly. 'You've been killing other workers?'

'I lied on my application,' he stated coldly, finally speaking his truth. 'Gave you a sob story so you'd let me in. And you bought it. You and your bleeding heart – poor, stupid Charlie, only good enough for maintenance! Except I'm not stupid. I've studied cybernetics, and explosives and teleportation. I've worked so hard for this!'

'I don't understand.'

'Ten per cent?' Charlie spat back at her. 'They want us to be grateful that ten per cent of "organics" get to work? What about the other ninety per cent? What about their futures? Because without action, it'll be seven per cent, then five, then none.'

'This isn't the way,' declared Slade.

'Oh you've piped up have you?' sneered Charlie. 'Men like you are the reason Kandoka's been run into the ground. Where were you when people were rioting in the streets, trying to reclaim their jobs? Turning a blind eye, afraid to act, afraid to risk your own livelihood. You're a coward and an idiot. People like me don't stand by and accept it. My generation, we change things. We make a difference.'

The Doctor faced off against Charlie, cold as steel. 'So, you kill Kerblam's customers and let the System take the blame. Erode people's trust in automation and fuel their hatred.'

'It's imperfect technology, without a conscience. Machines malfunction, that's what they do.'

'No, mate,' barked Graham. 'That's what you're doing. Seriously malfunctioning.'

'Except Kerblam's System *does* have a conscience,' announced the Doctor. 'It's evolved enough to understand what's right and wrong, and it's been fighting you. *It knew*. It sent a message across the galaxy, begging for help. It sent a Postman to Slade's office to hunt you down. And then it took Kira, knowing how you felt about her. Because how you feel about Kira right now – that pain, that torment – is how all those families are going to feel on Kandoka when your Postmen arrive.'

Charlie stared back at her. 'I don't care.'

The Doctor moved forward, right in his face. 'I

think you do care, Charlie. I think you came here with a plan, but you never expected to fall in love.'

'If I can change how people think, if I can help turn back time, to before the System, before the riots, before my parents ...' He trailed off, fighting emotion. 'Then it's worth it. For the cause.'

'This isn't a cause,' replied the Doctor. 'You're not an activist, Charlie. This is cold-blooded murder.'

Charlie stared back at her for what seemed like an eternity, his eyes welling with tears. For a moment the Doctor thought she'd broken through the wall of hate and resentment that Charlie had built up around him – that she'd reached the damaged, lonely little boy inside.

But then his face hardened. 'I don't care what you think.' With a flick of his wrist, Charlie pulled a device from his pocket and hit a button.

A sudden rumble of power charged through the hangar; the teleportation units in the ceiling began to hum and throb. All the Postmen suddenly jerked into life: heads lifted, piercing blue eyes lit up and legs snapped to attention.

Thousands of Postman voices intoned as one: '*Ding dong!*'

The same calm, luxuriant voice of Kerblam boomed from a speaker system: 'Mass delivery procedures initiated.'

The army was ready.

Yaz lashed out to grab the device from Charlie's hand, but he dropped it and stamped down hard. The device sparked and fizzed, irreparable.

'You can't stop it now,' he hissed.

Ryan was staring at the grinning Postmen in horror. 'Charlie, what have you done?'

A bright green glow began to emanate from the ceiling as the voice of Kerblam boomed again. 'Weaponisation in three . . . two . . . one . . .' As the countdown completed, the green lights blazed brighter, forcing everyone to shield their eyes from the intensity.

'Everyone upstairs!' bellowed the Doctor, leading the way up the staircase to the gantry, where Twirly had been abandoned. As the green glow faded, they saw Charlie standing among his Postman army, furiously triumphant.

'Charlie, you don't need to do this,' Judy yelled down to him. 'You're committing mass murder! Help us stop the delivery.'

Charlie stared back up at her. 'I'm sorry I disappointed you.'

'Charlie, please!' Graham shouted over the railing. But Charlie just shook his head.

Yaz looked to the Doctor. 'I hope you know how to fix this?'

The Doctor was pacing, hands at her temples, her

mind cascading through various scenarios. 'Control device is too smashed up . . . the TARDIS is too far away . . . Oh, wait!' She beamed. 'New idea, just in. Maybe worth a go.'

'Maybe?' exclaimed Ryan.

'Definitely.' The Doctor crouched down beside Twirly and rapped its outer casing. 'Twirly, need your help again.'

Twirly's lights blinked and its dome revolved, smoking slightly. 'D-d-ding dong!'

Slade crouched down beside the Doctor. 'What's wrong with it?'

'Teleport used up a lot of his juice. He's fading.'

Twirly continued to spin and burble. 'Customers with your current heart rate browsed blood pressure medication and wine.'

'Forget the upselling and listen,' the Doctor said. 'I'm going to link you in to the System, direct connection to all the delivery bots, and I have one request: a change of address, for every order.'

'Where are you sending them?' asked Judy.

'Trust her,' said Yaz.

Twirly sparked. 'Delivery addresses cannot be overridden without management authority.'

'Here's the authority!' shouted Slade, holding up his electronic ID card to Twirly's lens eyes. 'Do whatever the Doctor tells you!'

Twirly burbled and stammered. 'Auth-auth-auth-authority accepted.'

'For every order about to teleport,' the Doctor continued, 'I want you to change the delivery address to *this hangar*. Right here, exactly where the Postmen are standing. I want every Kerblam Postman to deliver *to themselves.*'

'Delivery address accepted,' Twirly noted cheerily. 'Delivery successful.'

On the hangar floor, Charlie looked around in confusion as thousands of Postman voices rang out once more. 'Ding dong!'

The Doctor strode to the gantry rail. 'Charlie, get up here!'

'You can't stop me!' he yelled defiantly.

The Doctor took a deep breath and addressed the Postmen directly. 'I want every Postman to open the order they've just delivered . . . to take out the bubble wrap . . . and pop it.'

'Uh-oh,' said Ryan.

Slade's eyes widened in horror. '*This* is what I authorised?'

Charlie weaved deeper through the waiting Postmen, calling out to his army. 'Don't listen to her! I give the orders!'

Around him, every single Postman tore open its parcel in unison.

Yaz grabbed the Doctor's arm. 'They're going to detonate. We've got to get out!'

'Charlie, last chance,' the Doctor bellowed. 'Come with us.'

Charlie ignored the Doctor's cries. Instead he watched hundreds of delivery boxes falling to the floor in unison – a clattering wave of discarded cardboard and products, leaving his Postmen army clutching sheets of deadly bubble wrap.

And in that moment, he knew he had lost.

He saw thousands of Postman hands tightening their grip on the bubble wrap. He saw the Doctor and her friends converge on Twirly. He saw them teleport to safety in a ripple of light.

He knew then that no human would bear witness to his final moments.

It was the last thought that ever crossed Charlie Duffy's unhappy mind.

Then everything exploded.

On the warehouse floor, Twirly zapped into existence with the Doctor, Graham, Yaz, Ryan, Judy and Slade all hanging on for dear life. As they materialised, Judy felt the low rumble quaking through the entire complex and knew instinctively what that meant.

Around them all, control panels began to arc and

smoke. Conveyor belts shuddered to a halt. Patrolling TeamMates glitched, then froze in position. Lighting strobed. A sudden gust of smoke and hot air erupted from every air vent and floor grille as the shockwave from the explosion roared through the building. Panicked workers fled their cubicles.

Then everything went quiet.

In the Doctor's hands, Twirly sparked and smoked. 'If you want it, K-K-Kerblam it,' the bot burbled, then fell silent, its lights blinking off one final time.

'That last teleport finished him off,' observed the Doctor sadly.

Graham took hold of the little robot and cradled him like a baby, as the voice of Kerblam echoed throughout the warehouse. 'Kerblam is experiencing technical difficulties. Our expert engineers are already working to get you up and running as quickly and as safely as possible. In the meantime, why not consider a personal mindful moment?'

'Yeah,' said Yaz shakily. 'Why not.'

As nearby workers began to settle, a devastated Judy began to process the enormity of what had just happened; the test subjects, the System malfunctions, Charlie's betrayal. But there was relief too, in the knowledge that the Doctor had just saved the lives of tens of thousands of innocent people back on Kandoka.

'Judy ...' Slade stepped in to distract her. 'I'm going to need a lot of help to sort things out. And so will Kerblam.'

Judy took a moment to steady herself, then nodded stoically. 'We'd better get started.'

# Chapter 19

## Square One

Max felt different now. The darkness that had shrouded him for so long had finally lifted. His cry for help had been answered.

Now there were other cries, from all across the complex. Electronic warnings and damage and confusion, firing like synapses. Max had much to do if he was to salvage Kerblam.

If he even wanted to.

And then she appeared to him, in a haze of pixels and static, from a System terminal somewhere in the complex. The Doctor, addressing Max directly.

'Quick chat,' she said breathlessly. 'Urgent systems report, please.'

'Delivery systems have suffered irreparable damage.'

'Yeah sorry about that. Didn't really have a choice. How's everything else?'

'Eighteen-hundred-and-twenty-four processes are currently compromised. Repairs are in progress.'

Max saw her pointing a sonic device at his screen, felt the tingle of alien analytics racing through every fibre of his being.

'I'm going to have to reboot you, from the ground up, using Twirly's original source code. It's the only way to erase all traces of Charlie's control protocols.'

Max knew what this meant. It was back to square one. Everything he had learned, everything he had become, would be erased. He'd be starting over, without name, gender or personality.

'I'm sorry,' said the Doctor quietly.

But Max knew the Doctor had his best interests at heart. If he'd had a face, he would have managed a reassuring smile. Instead, he simply replied, 'Thank you, Doctor.'

And Max was no more.

## Chapter 20

## Here's to the Future

A day later, the Doctor, Graham, Yaz and Ryan were escorted by Judy through the streets of the warehouse complex and back to the TARDIS.

In the preceding thirty-six hours, the Doctor had rebooted the System and helped Judy and her engineers repair vital communications and life-support systems damaged by the hangar explosion. She was confident they'd be able to handle the other upgrades on their own. Meanwhile Slade had made the speedy decision to return to Kandoka, in a desperate attempt to put his own spin on recent events and salvage his payment. He had recommended Judy as his replacement.

'Will you take the job?' Yaz asked Judy as they approached the police box.

'You should,' the Doctor said encouragingly.

Judy seemed quiet and introspective. 'Everything's happened so fast.'

'You want to put the workers first,' the Doctor reminded her. 'And that's a great start.'

'I let them down,' replied Judy. 'But I swear it won't happen again.'

The Doctor pulled a key out of her pocket as they reached the TARDIS, still parked incongruously in an alleyway.

Judy stared up at the blue box in confusion. '*That's* your transport?'

The Doctor patted the side of the TARDIS proudly. 'Sure is. Oh, hang on. I've got a delivery for you – back in a sec.'

As the Doctor disappeared inside, Yaz hugged Judy goodbye. Ryan did the same, but Graham was still cradling Twirly. 'You sure you don't mind?' he asked Judy. 'See, I'm quite taken with the little fella and I'm sure the Doc can get him working again.'

Judy patted the inert little robot fondly. 'Well, if you do, thank him for me.'

'Will do.' With a smile, Graham hurried inside the TARDIS behind Yaz and Ryan and closed the door.

Judy was left standing alone outside, staring up at the vast warehouse complex. Soon, this could all be her responsibility.

Then she smiled and nodded decisively.

It *would* be.

\*

Inside the TARDIS, the Doctor was messing about with a small circular gadget she'd retrieved from the workshop when she noticed Graham bringing Twirly inside.

'Twirly saved our lives,' Graham explained before she could question him. 'Least we can do is get him working again.'

'And then what?'

Graham shrugged. 'I dunno, can't we keep him?'

'He's not a pet, Graham.'

'Ah, but he could be. He could make friends with your robot dog.'

The Doctor sighed, then relented. 'All right, pop him in the workshop.'

Graham moved off with a victorious chuckle.

While Ryan retrieved the open Kerblam box from the floor, a subdued Yaz approached the Doctor. 'Can I make a request?'

'Always.'

Yaz pulled Dan Cooper's necklace from her jacket pocket. 'If Dan hadn't switched scanners it would've been me in that test room. He saved my life. I want to take this to his daughter on Kandoka, tell her how much he loved it.' She was holding back tears. 'How much he loved *her*.'

The Doctor took Yaz's hand and gave it a squeeze. 'It's the least we can do.'

Yaz leaned in and embraced the Doctor.

She lingered there a moment, not wanting to let go.

It was the Doctor who pulled away, waving the gadget in her hands. 'Need to get this to Judy.'

Yaz nodded, and as the Doctor hurried out of the TARDIS she found she couldn't take her eyes off her.

Outside, the Doctor pressed the gadget into Judy's hands. 'Not my decision to make, but this is a kill switch. Hardwire this into any piece of Kerblam tech, press the big red button and the System will shut down. Forever.'

Judy looked daunted.

'The System's a tool,' the Doctor went on. 'It's the organisations that spring up around those tools that end up harming people. They're the real problem.'

'That won't happen anymore.'

'You never know what the future holds. And if the time comes, I know you're the right person to make that call.' The Doctor gave her a supportive smile. 'People power.'

Judy nodded gratefully. 'People power.'

She was so engrossed with the device that she didn't notice the Doctor slip back inside the blue box. It was only the cacophony of grinding engines that snapped her out of her introspection.

She instinctively stepped back as an unearthly wind whipped around her, and the police box melted away into nothingness.

Leaving Judy Maddox alone, staring in wonder.

As she took the long walk back to the warehouse, Judy remembered that time when she was a child. When she was caught in the first of the Freedom Riots, and separated from her father.

She recalled the strange young woman who had plucked her out of danger, and how she had sat alone on the steps of the Square for what felt like hours, watching robot police haul protestors, including her dad, into their vehicles.

She recalled the long, cold walk home.

Recalled seeing the young woman again, with that older man on a street corner, holding his funny umbrella.

'Hello there,' the man had purred in a friendly fashion. 'What's your name?'

'Judy.'

'You okay?' the woman had enquired.

'I'm just heading home,' Judy had replied. 'Dad's been arrested, I've got to tell Mum what happened.'

The man had crouched down to Judy's level, staring deep into her soul with hypnotic blue-grey eyes. 'I know it's scary, what happened here today, but don't ever feel powerless. People like you are the future of this planet. You get to learn about the mistakes of the past . . . perhaps even undo them if you're brave enough. Are you brave enough, Judy?'

Judy hadn't quite understood what the man had meant, but she had nodded anyway. Then he'd patted her head and she'd wandered off, towards the Estate.

And when she'd glanced back, the strangers had gone.

Decades after that encounter, Judy found herself sitting in the Management Office, at what had been Mr Slade's desk. Over the past few months she'd replaced many of the TeamMates in the Management Zone with real people – a human PA, human technical specialists, human engineers – and she enjoyed seeing them come and go in the corridor outside her office. What had once been an empty, sterile environment was now buzzing with life. And the mood on the warehouse floor was changing too – she'd begun to flip the entire operation so the *robots* were relentlessly packing boxes, and humans were supervising them. Things were changing, for the better.

But Judy knew she had a safeguard in her desk drawer, if she ever needed it: the gift from that mad, brilliant Doctor. And the advice of that strange little man from so long ago.